Dangerous Decisions

Wolf Creek Pack Prequel

TJ Finn

TWO STRANGE CHICKS PUBLISHING

Dedication

This is dedicated to my two brothers, David and Michael. We made it through our childhood. There had been doubts but we did it. Love you both

Acknowledgements

I want to acknowledge my friends and family. Thank you for listening and nodding, even when you don't understand everything I'm talking about what I'm writing. That's how I know you love me LOL.

Chapter 1

Tessa

"What do you mean you're leaving? "Tessa blew a strand of hair out of her eyes as she carried her suitcase past Sean O'Reilly. He stood about halfway through her living room holding her daughter, Hannah. Sadness settled over her as she looked at the two of them, her throat tightening as she pushed back memories of a different time and place.

Swallowing hard, she shrugged at Sean's question. "I need a change, Sean. I have no family here now that my folks are gone. I have nothing to hold me down to this place." Tears burned in her eyes, and she took a deep breath to get her emotions under control.

"The pack is your family." He reached up to gently sweep Hannah's wild golden curls off her tiny forehead then looked back at Tessa. "I'm your family."

She gave up trying not to cry and let the tears fall this time. Moving closer to him, she wrapped one arm around him and the other around her daughter. Laying her head on his chest, she blinked back the tears. "You are my family, Sean, and I love you so much. But you of all people know what I mean. I need to move on, do something more with my life instead of living in the past and longing for what will never be." Lifting her head, she stepped back a little. "It's been three years."

They stood there, looking at each other. They were cousins and best friends growing up together, having fun, and creating chaos as only teenage shifters could. Tessa knew how hard it was going to be not having Sean constantly around, playing with Hannah, letting her lean on him. But her mind was made up.

Sean sighed and nodded reluctantly. "I understand, but I still don't like it."

Tessa gave him a soft smile and rubbed his arm. "I don't like it either, but I just can't stay. After meeting with my dad's lawyer, I found out they left me a hefty inheritance. I never knew they saved and invested like that, let alone went outside of the pack to do it. Oh, and life insurance." Tessa frowned. "What wolf takes out a life insurance policy, let alone one of that size?" Shaking her head, she went back into her bedroom for her other suitcase.

Seeing the picture of her parents on the table beside her bed, she picked it up and sat down. The picture had been taken a week before the accident that took them away from her. The other driver, driving a large SUV, had been drinking and fell asleep behind the wheel. When he swerved into oncoming traffic, he hit her parent's car head-on. The injuries they had sustained had been fatal, even for wolf shifters.

Wiping a tear away as it slid down her cheek, Tessa got up from the bed and slipped the picture into her overnight bag. Shouldering the bag and picking up her other suitcase, she walked back into the living room to see Sean on the floor with Hannah helping her stack blocks. Her little girl was going to miss her godfather.

Sean O'Reilly had been her rock the last three years since Hannah had been born. He checked on them every day, did work around the quaint little cottage her father had built himself. When Hannah was close to being born, they'd had a big snowstorm, but Sean and the pack enforcers were right there, shoveling everything so she could get the car if she needed to.

Sean had also been there for her. He had been there every step of the way when she discovered she was pregnant with Hannah. He had been her shoulder when things had gotten too much to bear. They were more than cousins. They were best friends and always would be.

"Ok, I think that's everything I'm taking. I just need to pick up Hannah's toys here in the living room, then we're good to go." Sean stood up and swept a giggling Hannah into his arms, hugging her tightly. Setting her back on her feet, he helped Tessa pick up all the toys and put them in a bag that Tessa would keep in the back seat of her old Durango.

The two of them carried everything outside and packed the suitcases and boxes in the back of the vehicle. Tessa lifted Hanna into her car seat, giving her some animal crackers and her favorite doll before closing her door. Turning, she collided with Sean, who had stepped close behind her. Tessa wrapped her arms around him tight, burying her face in his chest and started to cry. She was excited about the new phase of her life to start. Even though she didn't know where they were going to land or what was going to happen, she knew if she didn't leave then she would never move on.

"It's ok, Little Wolf." Sean whispered hoarsely into her ear and his words that were meant to comfort her only had her crying harder.

Tessa didn't know how long the two of them stood like that, holding each other, both of their hearts breaking until they pulled apart.

Sean reached out to wipe the last of her tears from her cheek and smiled. "It really will be ok, Little Wolf. Go out, find your way and know that I am always here for you, the pack is always here for you, if you decided to come home." She took a deep breath and nodded.

"I know, Sean. This will always be home, but I don't feel like I belong here anymore. I'll let you know when I get settled." Sean just nodded as he walked her to the driver's side door. Pulling her keys out of her pocket, she opened the door and climbed inside. She rolled down the window when she shut the door.

"Drive safe. That's my goddaughter in the back."

Tessa smiled at him and nodded. "No worries, Sean. I'll call when we stop for the night."

He stepped back as she started the vehicle then put it into reverse.

She slowly backed up, her eyes looking into the rearview mirror, then at the house. When she turned onto the highway, the quote she'd seen one day came to mind.

"There's a reason the windshield is bigger than the rearview mirror. Where you're going is so much better than where you've been."

Tessa certainly hoped so.

The vehicles in front of her inched slowly toward the flashing detour sign that told them all, again, that the road was closed ahead due to construction and to take an alternate route. She had been seeing this sign for miles and, like the drivers ahead of her, she had ignored them. Now, none of them had a choice. The road was closed and they either had to turn left or right. Problem was, she didn't know which way to turn.

The silence in the car had Tessa looking in the rearview mirror to check on Hannah. For the most part her daughter had been really good, but Tessa knew Hannah. She could go from happy to cranky in 2.4 seconds like her father. Her father. "God, now that was a man with mood swings. I wonder where he finally ended up-? Had he come to a Road Closed sign like she was about to and just drove until he found a place to land?

"Momma I'm hungry."

"Momma's hungry too, baby. I promise, the next place I see that serves food, I'll stop. Ok?"

"But I'm hungry now, momma."

Tessa rested her head on the back of her seat and sighed. And so it begins. "I'm hungry now too, Hannah but there's no where I can stop."

Hannah started crying, her little face set, not in sadness, but in anger. She threw her doll down on the seat beside her and, when Tessa stopped again, it slid onto the floor. That made the little girl even angrier and she started to kick the back of the seat in front of her. Tessa scrubbed a hand down her face, taking several deep breaths, letting each out very slowly as she tried not to lose her temper. It wouldn't do her any good to get upset too.

The detour was finally ahead of her and it was her turn to decide which direction they should go. Both directions looked the same. Both had rows and rows of corn on either side, but she could see hills further along and to the right. She sat there a moment, wondering what lay ahead and if Fate was done playing with her then. someone behind her honked their horn, causing her to jump. With a weary sigh, she started moving forward again then turned right.

"Mommy!! I am hungry!!" Hannah screamed as she kicked the back of the seat in front of her so hard it actually moved forward slightly. It was the growl that followed the scream that had Tessa slowing down and stopping on the side of the road.

Once she'd stopped, Tessa was able to pull together some grapes, cheese and yogurt for Hannah to eat. It was the same thing she'd given her right after they'd turned onto the road they were following now. Hoping that Hannah didn't shift while she was strapped in her car seat, Tessa pulled back onto the road, putting in one of Hannah's favorite CDs. The song Baby Shark started playing and her daughter started bouncing around to the tune while eating grapes.

Several hours later Hannah was asleep, and the vehicle was blessedly quiet. Tessa rubbed her eyes and stretched her neck. Her fingers were cramped from holding the steering wheel, and her legs ached from staying in the same position for so long. She never dreamed that they wouldn't find a place to stop and eat, then a clean motel. But, after four hours, there hadn't been anything except abandoned-looking gas stations and run-down farmhouses. She was getting worried that they wouldn't find anything.

The Durango jerked unexpectedly, and Tessa tightened her grip on the steering wheel. A moment later, she let out a breath and relaxed in her seat, loosening her grip when it continued to drive normally. Well, that had certainly woken her up.

When it jerked again, several lights lit up on her dashboard and the engine began to moan and rattle. She managed to pull over onto the side of the road before the vehicle finally stopped completely. Speechless, Tessa sat there a minute staring at the dashboard and tried to get it to start again, only stopping when the engine screeched at her in protest. Leaning back in her seat, she just sat there a moment, looking into the darkness

There was nothing but moonlight and cornfields surrounding them. Tessa stepped out of the Durango, taking care to not wake Hannah when she shut the door. Walking around to the front of the vehicle, she opened the hood. Using the flashlight on her cell phone, she looked at what lay before her. Well, there's the engine.

She had no mechanical skills and no idea how to even check the engine to see if she could find out what had happened. She hadn't ever actually fixed anything except her daughter's dolls. Sean or her father had always been there for anything major. She'd have to learn these things for the future.

Fear shot through her suddenly as she took another look around them. What a great place for an evil, sadistic man with an ax or a chainsaw to step out of the cornfields and either kidnap or kill them. Tessa just shook her head. She'd watched too many horror movies with Sean. Besides, she dared anyone to try and get between her and Hannah. There was nothing fiercer in the world than a momma wolf protecting her pup.

As the fear slid away, panic took a firm hold of her and her wolf paced. She hadn't seen a car in over a hundred miles, nor had she seen any houses with lights on in the middle of the damn cornfields. Her breathing became quick and shallow as she could feel herself teetering on the edge between logical thought and frantic imaginings. Her hand went to her throat and she took several deep breaths to calm herself. She would not panic. At least not while Hannah slept in her car seat.

Taking one more breath, she got back into her Durango and turned the flashlight feature off on her phone. She tried to get her GPS and map to work so she could figure out where the next town was. If anything, she could wait until it got lighter, put Hannah in her stroller, and start walking. Yes, she thought, feeling calmer, that's exactly what she'd do.

After several attempts to get her GPS to work, she realized she had no signal or internet service. The panic started to slowly seep into her bones again until she saw headlights coming up behind them.

Tessa jumped out of the vehicle and started waving her arms until the car finally slowed, then stopped beside them, the passenger window going down. An older gentleman dressed in overalls and wearing a tattered, dirty ball cap leaned over and looked at her.

"You're a long way from civilization, miss."

Tessa gave him a nervous smile, leaning in to speak to him. "Yes, I am. My car just stopped running, and I can't get it started. Do you know how far I am from the nearest town?"

The man nodded. "Grady is about forty miles up over that hill. I can take you there and you can get help." Tessa looked back at Hannah sleeping soundly then back to the man.

"I think I better stay here, but can you go there and let someone know to come to help me? Maybe the police or something?"

He looked past her to see what she had looked at then back to her. "You bet. I'll stop by the sheriff's office and he will send out the tow truck." Tessa smiled at him.

"Thank you so much. I'll just get in my Durango, lock the doors, and wait for help to come."

The man gave her a quick nod and the window slid up as he drove away. She jumped back into the Durango and locked the door. Patience was not one of her virtues, but she hadn't wanted to get into a stranger's car with her daughter. They would stay right there and wait for the cavalry to come.

Chapter 2

Jacob

Jacob let out the breath he was holding as he watched Lorna pace in front of him chewing her thumbnail, refusing to look at him. He hated that he had just hurt her and knew she was trying to decide how to respond to him. Suddenly she stopped pacing, her jaw clenched and trying to control her breathing.

"I have only one question left, Jacob."

They had been having a "discussion" for the past hour and a half and Jacob's brain was getting tired while his wolf paced restlessly. He wanted out. He wanted to run. But, despite the slight ripples in his muscles telling him his wolf was not happy, he'd been able to keep the animal contained. But it was 2:00 a.m. He needed to sleep. He wanted to go to sleep with Lorna curled up beside him. It didn't look like either were going to happen.

The argument, no she had called it a "discussion between two consenting adults", had started when Lorna told him she wanted to move in with him. She wanted to take their relationship to the next level, whatever the hell that meant. Jacob had been caught off guard. They had been in his bed, both lying there, trying to catch their breaths getting ready for round three...or was it four? He didn't know, all he knew was Lorna was sexy as hell with her long, tanned legs that perfectly wrapped around him, and her beautiful ebony hair that was long enough for him to wrap around his hand.

Lorna had asked and Jacob had said no. That should have been the end of it, but it hadn't been, and their "discussion" had been going on for the past hour and a half.

"Jacob, are you listening to me?"

Jacob blinked and focused on Lorna. He thought he had been listening but perhaps not. Perhaps he had been trying to control his wolf. Or maybe, his mind was just wandering because he was getting tired of "discussing" things.

"I am listening to you, Lorna." Liar. His heart sunk. "What is your question?" He knew what was coming. A question he was surprised hasn't been asked before now. Jacob braced himself. He hated hurting anyone, but he knew he was about to hurt Lorna.

"Do you love me? I don't think that you've ever said it back to me when I say it to you. You only smile and kiss me, and we move on."

Jacob quietly sighed and looked at Lorna. Any man would be lucky to love this woman. She was kind, caring, and intelligent. She wasn't clingy or demanding and was a wildcat in bed. Add all that together with how beautiful she was, and she had the total package. Most men would be flocking to her. But Jacob wasn't most men.

He stepped close to her and reached up to caress her beautiful olive skin. "I care for you, Lorna. We have fun, we enjoy each other's company. I like being with you." Jacob sighed. "I'm not in love with you, Lorna. We've talked about this. There's only one woman…"

Jacob stopped when he saw tears swimming in Lorna's dark blue eyes. He wanted to hold her, but he knew that he couldn't. She wiped a few stray tears from her cheeks as she nodded.

"I understand, Jacob. You're right, we have talked about this. But you two aren't together anymore and from what you've said, you won't ever be together again. Yet you can't seem to move on." Lorna wrapped her arms around herself and stepped back from him. "I can't be here anymore. I'm in love with you. Hopelessly, helplessly in love. I…"

Lorna was cut off when Jacob's phone started ringing. He ignored it and it stopped, then almost immediately rang again.

"Just answer it." Lorna sighed, waving her hand toward his phone.

Jacob picked up his phone.

"Yeah?" He growled out the greeting, not happy to be interrupted.

"Jacob, it's Max."

"Yeah, I have caller ID." Jacob watched Lorna walk out of the kitchen and to his bedroom. "What do you need, Max? It's almost 3:00 a.m."

The Sheriff chuckled at his tone. "Just had Paul Simpson stop by the station to say that there is a woman and her kid broke down on Highway 93 around mile marker 42. She declined his offer to drive them into town with him, so he wanted to make sure I knew. Can you get your truck and head out there?"

He glanced at the clock on his stove. What the hell was a lone woman with a kid doing traveling this late at night in an unreliable vehicle?

"Yeah. Let me put some clothes on and I'll head out."

"Yes, please put some clothes on. We don't want to scare the poor woman any more than she probably is."

"Fuck you, man. I'm a fine specimen of a man. Every woman in town wants to see my naked ass."

Jacob immediately regretted his words when Lorna walked back into the kitchen, fully dressed, her keys in her hand. The pained look on her face had his chest tightening and he dropped his arm, pulling the phone away from his ear.

"Lorna, I…"

"Don't. Just don't Jacob. I'll be back in a couple days to get my stuff. Goodbye."

He watched her walk out the back door, the screen door banging shut behind her. Shaking his head, he brought the phone to his ear again. "Max…"

"Sorry, man. I didn't think. Did I interrupt something? Is Lorna there?"

Jacob let out a long sigh. "Lorna's not here. At least not anymore. We just broke up."

"Seriously? Ah man, I'm sorry. Was it mutual?"

Jacob didn't want to talk about it, but he and the Sheriff were best friends and he knew Max was just trying to help. "Not really sure to be honest, and I really don't want to talk about it. I'm going to hang up so I can dress and get out there before the woman starts to panic."

"Alright, but we're going out for a few beers later, and you're gonna tell me what happened."

Jacob knew that was not going to happen. He wasn't going to tell him or anyone what happened. That wasn't fair to Lorna. "I'm hanging up now Chatty Cathy. I've got work to do. Oh, and Max? Give Willow my best."

He ended the call before the Sheriff could say anything else and headed into his bedroom. He'd move on and do what was needed to be done. Pulling on a pair of jeans and a t-shirt, he grabbed his leather coat and keys before heading out to rescue a stranded woman.

He drove through the sleepy little town of Grady, heading out onto the state highway that ran through the middle of town. Max had told him mile marker 42. It would take him about half an hour, so Jacob slipped his favorite AC/DC CD into the player and turned up the music.

The beat thrummed through his whole body and all the tension eased from his shoulders to the point he felt lighter. The headache that the argument caused was loosening its hold on his head.

He had told Lorna the truth. He wasn't in love with her because someone else had taken his heart, and he knew it would always belong to her. It didn't matter that it had been three years since he'd seen her. He and his wolf had known she was their fated mate early on and there wouldn't be anyone else to fill her spot.

As Jacob topped the only hill on the highway for almost a hundred miles, he could see the vehicle on the side of the road, its hood up and a woman sitting inside doing something with her cell phone. The light of the phone sent a soft glow over her face, but he was still too far away to make out any features. All he could see was her bowed head as she looked down at it. Pulling his truck to the side of the road, he slowly approached the vehicle so that the front end of both faced each other.

He climbed out of his truck, grabbing his toolbox and flashlight, and walked to the Durango to look down at the engine. The driver's side door opened, then closed and the woman walked around with him. The familiar scent of honeysuckle and pine hit him as she stopped next to him. His wolf whimpered and paused suddenly, taking Jacob by surprise. She spoke and he knew why.

"It just stopped. I gassed up about a hundred miles back, and it was driving just fine. Then suddenly it jerked and rocked. It kept going for maybe another mile, then jerked again and stopped. I haven't been able to get it to start again."

All the air in Jacob's lungs whooshed out as his heart started racing so hard and so fast, he thought his heart would explode from his chest. He stepped back and shined his flashlight into her face. The familiar small rounded nose had the same splash of freckles and dark green eyes looked up at him, wide and questioning. His wolf whimpered again, but Jacob pushed him back. That earned him a growl as his muscles rippled. The damn beast wanted out right then and there. But who could blame him?

"Do you mind? You're blinding me."

"Tessa?" His throat had tightened, and he'd had to force the name out of his mouth. The woman tilted her head the same way he always remembered and looked at him.

"How do you know me?" She took a step away from him, her tone had lowered and sounded as menacing as she could get. He knew that tone. It was the one she used before she'd start kicking ass and taking names. She had been his little firecracker, his Little Wolf...his. He turned the flashlight around to shine it on his face just enough so she could see him. She took two more steps back.

"Jacob?" Now her voice seemed breathless and she quivered when she said his name.

"Yeah. What the hell are you doing in the middle of Illinois?"

Before she could say anything, a tiny voice called to her from inside the vehicle and, after one last frowning look at him, she hurried to the back passenger door and opened it. Jacob walked around the hood of the vehicle in time to see her leaning in, one foot off the ground as she handed something back to a little girl sitting in a booster seat. He frowned and walked closer, standing behind her and looking down. Yep, there was the same perfect ass sticking up in the air. He itched to reach out and run his hand over it, then around her waist to pull her up to him. Instead, he clenched his fist and spoke.

"When did you have a baby?"

Tessa slid out of the back seat and quickly closed the door. She stood toe to toe with him, her stubborn chin jutted up, her dark red hair falling away from her face and her eyes blazing. "Hannah turned three two weeks ago."

Jacob's shoulders stiffened as he leaned down and tried to see the child. It had been a little over three years since he'd left Colorado and the pack that had been his home and family. Left? More like run out of town and banned from the only people he knew and loved. Banned from being with his fated mate. His wolf growled at that, and he pushed him back again.

"Is she…" His heart thumped wildly in his chest at the implications of the next word he wanted to say. "Mine?"

Tessa put her hands on her hips and jutted her chin out even more, if that were possible, her eyebrows knitting together as she gave him a hard look. "Hannah is my daughter."

He raised an eyebrow. "…And where is her dad?"

He watched sadness wash over her face and heard her take a deep, shuddering breath. "He's gone. I haven't seen him since before she was born. So, back off, Bubba, and see if you can fix my Durango so we can get back on the road."

Chapter 3

Tessa

Tessa pushed open the door and led Hannah into the motel room she had just paid cash for. Hannah ran inside, pushing the door wider so she could follow her daughter inside carrying their overnight bag, kicking the door closed behind them. Tessa was exhausted, her shoulders felt like they were clear up to her ears, and her head hurt. Did wolves get headaches? It was either a headache or a tumor. At that moment, she would prefer the tumor over a headache. It would be a good excuse not to see Jacob again.

Hannah crawled onto the queen-sized bed, sitting in the middle of the small room and started jumping on it. Tessa gave her daughter an indulgent smile as she dropped the bag onto the floor with a loud thump. Pulling her phone out of her pocket, she checked to see if she'd gotten any calls, then laid it on the small writing desk opposite the bed before looking around the room.

Thankfully, the room looked clean and quaint with cream-colored curtains and dark brown carpeting. Sitting on the edge of the bed, she ran her hand over the handmade quilt, then closed her eyes and fell backward, laying an arm over her eyes. The bed dipped gently beside her before she felt her daughter's hand moving softly over her forehead. Smiling at Hannah's gently feathery touch, she opened her eyes. "You ok, momma?"

"Momma's tired, sweet pea. That's all." The pounding behind her eyes made the statement a lie, but her daughter didn't need to know that. Truth be told she was tired, hungry, and confused which, combined, made for one big headache.

When Jacob had shined the flashlight on his face, her knees had gone weak and her wolf had gone crazy. In a rush of emotions, every memory and feeling she'd worked three years to get over, hit her all at once. His eyes were still the dark brown they'd always been and his lips full and inviting. When he'd frowned at her, he still had the little crease between his eyes that she used to tease him about.

Tessa couldn't remember a day in her life that Jacob hadn't been there. The two of them, along with her cousin, Sean, had grown up together and had all been best friends. Then, one day, when they were seventeen and Sean wasn't with them, they went from being best friends to realizing they were fated mates.

Jacob had stolen a kiss from her, and something seemed to suddenly shift in both of them—it wasn't just their wolves. Fate had taken over. A year later, on a warm, sunny Spring day, they mated. All they would need to do was to stand before their Pack, in the sacred circle and recite the words that would bind them both together forever. Her father, on the other hand, was less than amused by their mating, saying they were too young, and he would not give his consent for them to take the final step until she was older.

Tessa felt a weight on her chest as if someone had stacked bricks on top of her. That was all before Sean's dad died. The elders had asked if anyone wanted to challenge Sean as the alpha. According to Pack law and ritual, he couldn't just take the role of Alpha. He had to fight for it. No one stepped forward. That was until Jacob, without even telling her, declared his intentions at a Pack gathering.

Tessa had begged Jacob to reconsider. They all knew the consequences of losing a challenge for Alpha. No matter the outcome, she would be the one to lose. But he pushed forward with his plan and when he'd lost and was banished, it had taken her father, Sean, and a couple of Pack Enforcers to stop her from running after him.

Tessa hadn't seen Jacob again and she'd slid into a deep depression, unable to look at her father or, at times, to even be in the same house with him. Sean had tried to get to her, but she'd refused to see him. She'd gotten sick and her depression had deepened. After four more days of not being able to keep anything down, her mother forced her to the pack doctor who declared that she was going to have a pup of her own. Tessa had finally reached out to Sean and they'd picked up where they'd left off. Later, the two had brought Hannah into the world and had raised her together, until now.

"Momma, I'm hungry." Tessa smiled at her and sat up.

"Ok, sweet pea. Let's walk over to the little diner across the street, then we'll come back and sleep a little bit." Hannah nodded and slid off the bed as Tessa stood.

Slipping her tiny hand into Tessa's she tugged on her mother's arm. "Will you be sleeping too?"

Tessa nodded as she led her daughter outside, the door closing and locking behind them. "You can bet I will be. I'm almost as tired as I am hungry."

Mother and daughter hurried across the street to the diner, finding a booth to sit in. The waitress put a piece of paper with images for Hannah to color and some crayons and Tessa smiled her thanks. Handing Hannah a couple of crayons, Tessa looked around, catching several people glancing over at the then talking in low hushed tones to each other.

The waitress came back, bringing a cup of coffee and a glass of milk, then took their orders. Once she left, Tessa did her best to distract her daughter. She didn't want Hannah to know that people were staring and talking about them. Tessa didn't blame them. They were strangers, after all.

Loud knocking on the hotel room door bought Tessa out of a deep, troubled sleep. She'd been dreaming that Jacob had discovered Hannah was his daughter and had taken her away. She chased them, never quite catching up to them. She looked at her phone, then at her daughter sleeping like an angel and covered her with the blankets she'd kicked away in her sleep.

Tessa got up and was yawning when she opened the door to find Jacob standing there in loose, greasy jeans and a tight-fitting t-shirt that had her heart stopping and her breath hitching. It wasn't until her heart slammed into her chest that she took a breath and looked up at him. God the man was sexy even when he was dirty. Maybe especially when he was dirty.

"Hey." Sleep hung heavily in her voice

Jacob grinned at her, and heat creeped into her cheeks as she smoothed her tangled mess of hair down, even though she knew it wouldn't help.

"Hey yourself. You guys got some sleep. Good."

"Is my Durango fixed?" Jacob let out a breath and put his hand in his back pocket.

"Well, about that. I can't get the parts for it for a couple of days. Also…"

He pulled his hand out of his back pocket and pulled out a piece of paper, holding it out to her. "When I ordered the parts and used the credit card information you gave me, it was declined.

Tessa frowned and took the piece of paper he held out to her. "Declined? It couldn't have." She turned from the door and went to the desk to get her cell phone. Finding the number to her parents' attorney, she called it and waited as it rang several times. The voicemail answered.

"Mr. Charles, its Tessa Cafferty. I just tried to use my credit card that's connected to the account we set up and it was declined. Please call me back as soon as you can. My Durango broke down, and I need to pay for parts and labor. Thanks." Tessa ended the call and slipped her phone in her back pocket, turning to Jacob feeling embarrassed. "Um, there's no reason why it should have been declined."

Heat crept into her cheeks when she saw that Jacob watched her closely as he leaned against the doorframe. "Well, I covered the parts and, as I said, they'll be here in a couple of days. Do you have enough cash to stay here for another three or four days?"

Tessa looked at him wide-eyed, not answering him for a moment. She only had another hundred dollars in cash and that wouldn't cover the hotel room that long. Jacob straightened and started to reach into his back pocket, and she raised a hand.

"No, I can't take your money. I'll figure something out."

Jacob's eyebrow shot up and he crossed his arms, looking down at her. She felt her cheeks warm at his look and tucked her tangled mess of curls behind her ear, her chin jutting up defiantly. "I mean it, Jacob. I'm not taking money from you. I…"

She was cut off by the ringing of her phone and she quickly fished it out of her pocket, turning her back on him as she answered it. "Mr. Charles. Thank you for calling me back so quickly."

"Of course, Miss Cafferty. I took a few minutes to make some calls about the credit card. Are you traveling?"

Tessa frowned and glanced at Hannah a moment. "I am. I'm traveling to Maine to see if it might be a good place to live with Hannah.

"Why?"

"I see. I wish you would have told me, but, of course, neither of us could have known it would be an issue."

She looked at Jacob over her shoulder, then turned away from his concerned look. "What issue?"

"It seems that the system recognized that there were purchases made outside of your normal purchasing area and automatically locked down the account."

"My account is frozen? It's frozen because a computer didn't recognize where I was spending money?" It was hard to keep her voice and panic down so she wouldn't wake her daughter. "Mr. Charles, I'm stuck in a town in the middle of Illinois. My Durango broke down and I need those funds to pay for repairs and a hotel until its fixed and food for my daughter!"

"I understand, Miss Cafferty, and I wish there was something I could do. The earliest that I can contact a live person is Tuesday. Monday is a bank holiday."

The rug wasn't being pulled out from under her, the whole damn floor was breaking apart under her feet, and she had nothing to hang on to. Her throat tightened as frustrated tears filled her eyes. "Thank you, Mr. Charles. Please let me know if you hear anything sooner."

Tessa disconnected the call and just stared at the phone a moment, then closed her eyes as a tear fell down her cheek. Shaking her head, she set her phone on the desk and lifted her head to look at the ceiling. "Don't you think you've thrown enough at me, God? Don't you think I deserve to start a new life and be happy?" She knew not to ask that question but didn't know what else to do.

Chapter 4

Jacob

Jacob stepped into the motel room, shutting the door behind him when Tessa turned her back on him to take the phone call. He should have been the gentlemen, respected her privacy, shut the door and waited for her to let him back in. But he wasn't a gentleman by any means and to hell with privacy. He wanted to know what was going on.

He looked at the bed and studied the little girl wrapped up in a blanket hugging a stuffed, black wolf to her chest. She had her mother's wild curly hair, but, instead of red, it was a dark brown. When he'd seen her last night, his heart stopped, and his thoughts had gone wild with possibilities. Was she his? He'd wanted to get a good look at her face, but Tessa stepped between them, had become the fierce, protective mother wolf, and had shut the door so the light turned off inside.

After he dropped them off at the motel, then towed their vehicle to his shop, he'd gone home and tried to get a few more hours of sleep. All he ended up doing was lying in the dark thinking about Tessa and wondering what twist of fate had brought Tessa Cafferty back into his life. Memories of the two of them and what they'd had together still haunted him even after three years.

It took almost a year for him to stop thinking of Tessa every minute of every damn day. He'd left his home and the pack lands so fast the two of them hadn't been able to say goodbye. There had been no time for him to beg her to come with him and promise her that the dreams they could still come true. No, Pack enforcers escorted him home so he could pack his things. He'd tried to sneak out once, but the damn wolves were all around his house caught him immediately. His heart hurt so bad that he could barely sit straight on his bike when he drove away.

Tessa disconnected her call and turned to look at Jacob. Her face was flushed, and tears lingered on her lashes. It about killed him. All he wanted to do was pull her into his arms and kiss her, tell her everything would be ok.

"Come on, Little Wolf. Get your stuff together. I can't fix the bank issue, but I can help lessen the burden."

Instead of kissing her, he reached out to brush the tears away, but she stepped back from him. "What do you mean?"

"I have a big house with several empty bedrooms upstairs I never use. There's even a master suite of sorts that connects with a smaller bedroom by a bathroom. You can keep the doors open and hear Hannah if she needs you and stay out of my way at the same time." His lips twitched at that then disappeared when she shook her head so hard her curls whipped around her face and stepped farther back.

"I can't stay with you." She squealed.

Jacob sighed and walked over to the things she had laid out for both her and Hannah and shoved them into the overnight bag. Tessa hurried over pushing him and zipped the bag up, but not before he spotted the dark red thong and bra laying on top of everything. He almost growled out loud. That would haunt him the rest of the day.

"We are not staying with you. I don't even know you anymore. You're a stranger and I'm not subjecting Hannah to someone I barely know."

A dark look crept over his face and he took a menacing step forward. "Are you saying I'd hurt a child? I'd hurt your daughter?"

Tessa swallowed. He could see the vein in her neck pulsing and could smell a hint of fear. Raising his head slightly, he breathed in before another smile tugged at his lips. He could also smell her desire. That was his. He had done that to her.

"No, of course not, Jacob." She opened her mouth as if she was about to say something else, then closed it as she shook her head. "No. I'm sorry. I'm not thinking clearly at the moment."

"Glad to hear that you don't think I'd do that." He walked past her and picked up the bag "Now, this is a small town in the middle of nowhere USA. We have two motels, and this is the better of the two. There are no bed and breakfasts or anything like that. Once you reach 11:00 a.m. tomorrow, you will be out on the street with your little girl. I'm trying to help you avoid that."

Jacob walked to the door, then turned back to her. He nearly laughed at her look as she stood there watching him. "Grab Hannah. It's still early in the day. Enough time to run by the shop, get the rest of your things, then get you back to my place. The two of you can get settled and I'll get back to work while the two of you get a little more sleep. You look like you're about to fall back to sleep standing there."

Jacob closed the hood of the car he'd just finished working on, wiped his hands on a rag, then walked to his office. Dropping into the dirty leather chair behind his desk, he let out a tired breath. He'd been working for the last three hours, but he couldn't take his mind off the momma wolf and her pup sleeping upstairs at his house. He kept picturing her wearing that red bra and thong as he touched her in ways he used to. At one time she had been a thin little sprite who he loved and wanted more than he had wanted to breathe. No, this time he saw the curves of the woman she had become and all he wanted was to run his hands over every curve.

Jacob scrubbed a hand over his face. He'd been around her less than twenty-four hours and already he wasn't sure he'd be able to keep his hands, or his fantasies, to himself. Looking at the clock, he spit out a few profanities when he saw how late it was.

Standing, Jacob went through the shop, closing everything down, then got his bike. As he turned onto the road heading toward his place, he hoped he could handle an evening with Tessa with this sudden, overwhelming need to claim her. Then a thought occurred to him. There would be no way that Tessa could hide the little girl from him now. He would get to see her, talk to her, and perhaps figure out if the little girl was his.

The sun was just starting to set when he pulled into his driveway and into his garage. The smell of propane wafting in from the backyard was enough to make Jacob's stomach rumble from hunger. Swinging his leg over the bike, he walked to the door that lead to the backyard and stopped. Tessa chasing her daughter around his backyard while Hannah's laughter mixed with Daughtry coming from unseen radio.

When Tessa caught Hannah and swung up the giggling toddler into her arms, mother and daughter throwing their heads back with laughter, Jacob's legs nearly stopped holding his big frame. He put his hand against the door to hold himself steady, but his eyes never left the two. His throat tightened and his vision blurred as the long-forgotten sadness filled him. They'd been robbed of all their dreams—of a life just like this. He and Tessa had talked long into the night about the life they would have, the children that would fill their home, then the grandchildren that came after.

"Jacob?" It took him a moment to register that Tessa was talking to him. He shook his head to clear away the sadness and looked at Tessa holding Hannah. It was then he saw it. The resemblance was uncanny with the same dark eyes, the way one side of Hannah's mouth lifted first before she gave him a full smile.

Jacob pulled his eyes away from his daughter and looked at Tessa. "I'm sorry. What?"

Tessa frowned and shifted Hannah in her arms before she spoke again. "I said welcome home and asked if the steaks were ok because I'd already set some out and started the grill."

"Yeah." He nodded his head and looked at Hannah again. Tessa looked between Jacob and Hannah then nodded toward Jacob. "Hannah, this is mommy's friend Jacob. He's also a friend of Uncle Sean's."

Jacob frowned at the mention of Sean then watched when Hannah laid her head on Tessa's shoulder, her eyes never leaving Jacob. He gave her a warm smile and nodded. "Hi Hannah."

Hannah wiggled in Tessa's arms until she set the little girl down. "She's not met many people she doesn't know. Once she gets to know you, she'll never stop talking."

Tessa crouched down in from the little girl. "Sweetie, why don't you go find your wolf and get the pink sweater I set on your bed. It's getting chilly." Hannah nodded, again, her eyes never leaving Jacob until she finally turned and ran into the house as fast as her little legs would carry her.

When Tessa straightened, she wouldn't meet his eyes at first, but he didn't move. He just stood there watching as she chewed on her bottom lip and looked at the door Hannah had run through. He wanted to be the one to chew that lip, nip at her neck, run his hand over her smooth skin. When she turned, he gave her a long, steady look before he spoke.

"I'm going to go take a shower and when I get back, perhaps you'd like to explain why you lied to me."

Tessa's frown deepened. "How did I lie to you?"

His eyebrow shot up, then he tucked his chin, his dark eyes never leaving hers. "You lied when you told me Hannah wasn't my daughter."

Chapter 5

Tessa

Tessa tucked Hannah into bed, and she was asleep in minutes without even the two of them reading the Beatrix Potter series, The World of Peter Rabbit. Tessa sat there a moment, tucking the blanket around her daughter, watching her sleep. Yes, she was putting off going back downstairs. Putting Hannah to bed was the out she'd needed to get away from Jacob, hopefully putting an end to their evening. Maybe, when she headed back down to clean up, she would find him gone or in bed.

Fat chance, Tessa thought as she quietly left Hannah's room. She knew Jacob, or at least she had known him, and she didn't imagine he had changed that much in three years. Not only hadn't he left or gone to bed, she knew he was waiting for her to come down. He would probably come up to look for her if she didn't go down there soon. Besides, she could handle herself. Yes, she might owe him the whole truth, but she would not be bullied into anything and Jacob could be a big bully sometimes.

Taking a deep breath, Tessa headed downstairs, glancing around the empty living room, then moved to the empty kitchen. Perhaps she was wrong. Maybe Jacob had gone to bed or, better, maybe he'd gone out with the boys. Tessa frowned. Did he have any "boys" to go out with? She sighed as she went to the sink and opened the dishwasher door.

There had been a time when she knew everything about Jacob and could even predict what he was thinking. There had also been a time that she was the focus of his entire world as he had been hers. Even after he was banished, she just knew he'd figure a way to get back to her and take her away with him.

He hadn't come and, after she'd cried all the tears she could, she had hated him for not coming. That was until she had realized she was pregnant. How could she hate him when he had left the most beautiful gift anyone could give her? Tessa and Sean had searched for him then but had come up with nothing. So, she had given birth to his daughter, named her after his mother then raised her with the help of Sean as her Godfather and had tried to give their daughter the life she thought he would want her to have.

She had finally given up on ever finding him after three years and tried to shut down every emotion she had for him. Fate, it seems, had something else in mind. For all of them.

Tessa shook those thoughts out of her head and finished cleaning the kitchen. There was a lot of food left that she had to put into the fridge as she went. Tessa had been too nervous and too tense to eat. They had kept the conversation light, listening to Hannah talk about everything she had seen today. After dinner, Tessa had taken her daughter upstairs for a bath then bedtime. She looked around the kitchen, finally satisfied that she had put everything away.

Glancing at the clock it was 8:00 but still no Jacob. Good. Perhaps she would go up to her bedroom, take a bath in the beautiful claw-foot tub, and go to bed herself. She was still feeling sleep-deprived and hopefully she'd have good news tomorrow.

Tessa started to turn off the kitchen light when she heard something in the garage. She stared at the back door a moment, chewing on her lip trying to decide if she should go see what it was, then shook her head and headed out. What if someone was trying to steal something while Jacob was gone, and she did nothing about it? The garage door that lead into the backyard was open, and a light was on. She was halfway to the garage door when she heard Jacob's voice and she stopped then turned around. If she hurried, she could get back inside and up to her room before he knew she was out there.

She was almost to the backdoor when she heard his deep chuckle and turned around. He stood there, leaning against the door frame in a pair of tattered jeans that hung loosely on his hips and no shirt. Her eyes went instantly to his chest and the memory of the days she'd licked and kissed every inch of it.

"Chicken." His voice had her looking up at him, heat creeping into cheeks.

"What?" Tessa wasn't sure she'd heard him correctly since she hadn't really been paying attention. Damn those abs.

Jacob pushed away from the door, sticking the rag he had in his hands into his back pocket and walked toward her. "I called you a chicken. Did you think we wouldn't continue the conversation about you lying to me about Hannah?"

Tessa's chin jutted up, and she crossed her arms, anger starting to fill her. "How did I lie, Jacob?"

He grinned and shook his head as he stopped in front of her. Tessa had to look up at him since she was barefoot and the heat that was coming off him washed over him. The scent of grease mixed with his natural musky pine scent invaded her senses completely.

"I asked you if she were mine and you told me no. All it had taken was one good long look at her eyes and her face and I knew she was mine. She has my eyes, she looks like my mother, and she has my mother's name."

Their gazes locked then Tessa looked away and stepped back from him. In one step, Jacob reached her, his hand gripping her chin, forcing her to look up at him. "Tell me the truth, Tessa. I know it but I need to hear you say it."

Jacob's grip on her chin prevented her from looking away or even moving away from him so she straightened her shoulders, fire flashing in her eyes, and gritted her teeth as she spoke.

"Let go of me, Jacob." She tried to jerk her head free but failed.

"Not until... humph..."

Tessa punched Jacob, catching him off guard enough that he let her go. That left her free to punch him again, this time in the jaw, making him stumble back enough that she turned to hurry into the house.

Tessa's one thought was to get her daughter and lock the door to her bedroom, staying in there until she could call her lawyer in the morning, get her money, and get the hell out of town. Two strong arms banded around her and pulled her back against Jacob's hard body. She struggled until he tightened his hold on her, his warm breath brushing through her hair as he spoke into her ear. "Where are you running to, Little Wolf? Why are you fighting? Just say the words and I'll let you go, and you can run up and protect Hannah from the big bad wolf."

Electricity pricked at her skin and down her spine at the feel of his warm voice on her cool skin and all her anger left her when he called her Little Wolf in that deep sexy voice of his. Tessa shivered even as warmth washed over her. Closing her eyes, she was aware of his body against hers, how they molded together perfectly, and how it felt to just have his arms around her again, even if it was in anger. Liquid heat rushed through her, pooling between her legs. The need to feel his hands and mouth on her like he'd done before their entire world had disintegrated around them was almost overwhelming.

"Jacob..." Her voice was a hoarse plea, but she didn't think he heard her until he whispered in her ear.

"Please, Tessa."

Tessa closed her eyes, laying her head back against his chest. "Yes, Jacob. Hannah is yours."

The words hung in the air between them and, to Tessa, it felt as if the entire world stopped, neither one of them breathing. The temperature felt as if it dropped several degrees and she actually shivered as the cool air hit her heated skin when he stepped away from her. Turning around, she saw the look of shock and disbelief on his face. He scrubbed a hand down his stubbled jaw and his eyes bore into her.

Her chest tightened at the look he was giving her three years of pain and suppressed feelings flashing over his features. "Did you know..."

Tessa shook her head as her eyes filled with tears. "No. I didn't find out for over a month after you'd left. I thought it was depression and…"Her voice hitched. "…heartbreak." A tear slowly slid down her cheek before she continued. "I waited for weeks for you to sneak back and take me away with you."

He closed his eyes at that, dropping his head a moment, before opening them again, anguish and regret reflecting in them.

"It's ok, Jacob. I know now that you couldn't. Sean had told me that the pack enforcers were watching me and your place carefully for almost six months after they banished you."

Jacob nodded then stepped closer to her, wordlessly reaching out to her. Her breath hitched as she closed the distance, stepping into his arms. Pulling her against his hard chest, he buried his face in her hair as her tears started and she quietly sobbed. They had all been robbed of so much. Hannah had been robbed of a family, and she and Jacob had been robbed of their love.

Tessa lifted her head from Jacob's chest when she felt him straighten and looked up at him, her eyes swimming in tears. In that one moment, there was just the two of them. The world around them ceased to exist, leaving only the memories of what had once been between them. Tessa's eyes dropped to his lips, remembering every single kiss they had shared, and her lips parted, her tongue darting out to run along her bottom lip. A low growl rumbled in Jacob's chest and her eyes moved back to his.

Before she knew what was happening, Jacob kissed her, his lips pressing against hers, his tongue licking across her bottom lip until she opened for him. Their tongues brushed against each other in a slow, familiar dance that was both tentative and teasing. She moaned softly as his hands pressed against her back, molding her against him. Her hands moved up his chest, feeling his muscles ripple and jump beneath her touch until she wrapped her arms around his neck, her fingers brushing through his hair.

At that moment, she felt as if everything that had been wrong had been righted, and all the struggles she had gone through since losing him, having Hannah, and losing her parents were now behind her. It felt like she had finally found her place in a world that had tried to tear her down and the darkness that had threatened to consume her had been pushed back by the light of her love for Jacob.

Chapter 6

Jacob

Jacob's mind catapulted into memories he had tried to keep buried for three years. He'd tried to forget just how perfect Tessa's body fit his, the sexy little sounds she made when he kissed her. Hell, even the sound of the cute little snore she had when she slept, hit him like a brick wall. His mind might have forgotten, or tried to forget, all the things that had made him love his Little Wolf, but his heart never did. From this one kiss, everything inside him that had felt broken, fell into place where it all belonged.

He growled low in his chest and his kiss turned possessive. Moving his hands down her back, he cupped her ass before settling onto her hips. Lifting her, she instinctively wrapped her legs around his waist and they both moaned from the feel of her grinding against his hard shaft.

Tearing his mouth from hers, he nipped his way across her jaw and down to her neck while her fingers brushed through his hair. He reached the point where her delicate neck met her beautiful, strong shoulders, a place he knew drove her wild, and smiled against her skin when her head fell back with a soft moan from her swollen lips.

His tongue lavished her silky, smooth skin, sucking on that delicate junction that held his mark. Pain twisted in his heart for a moment, but it slipped away when he heard her whisper his name, the sound of it swirling in the surrounding air. It was something he never thought he'd ever hear again. She said his name again, and he lifted his head, looking at her, cheeks flushed, and her lips swollen from being kissed. He'd never seen her more beautiful. That was until she opened her soulful, dark brown eyes, heavy with passion, and looked at him.

"I need you, Jacob. Please."

He closed his eyes a moment. If this was all a dream, he never wanted to wake up. When he opened them again, a smile slowly spread across her lips. He moved her in his arms so quickly, she yelped in surprise. He kissed her again then tossed her over his shoulder, smacking her ass when she started to protest.

Wordlessly, he carried her into the house, kicking the back door closed behind him, then through the kitchen. Tessa started laughing and wiggling again. "Put me down Jacob."

Entering the bedroom, Jacob smacked her ass again before tossing her onto his large bed, grinning down at her as she continued laughing and bounced. "I've missed that laugh, Little Wolf." Yanking his shirt over his head, he leaned over, placing his hands on either side of her as her smile slowly slipped away, her eyes moving to his lips then back to his eyes.

"No one could make me laugh like you did, Jacob. I've missed it too."

Tessa sat up, her eyes starting to turn the light amber of her wolf's eyes. She lifted her t-shirt over her head and tossed it to the floor, then started taking off her bra, but Jacob dropped to his knees in front of her and covered her hands with his.

"Mine." Slowly he unhooked her bra, his eyes never leaving hers. He couldn't breathe for a moment as her beautiful breasts tumbled into his hands. Her breath hitched and her dark pink nipples grew harder when he brushed his thumbs over them. They had always fit perfectly in his hands. His thumbs brushed across her hardened nipples. Everything about her had fit him perfectly. Looking up at her, his hands moved slowly over her delicate skin to push her bra completely off her shoulders then let his fingers dance along her skin until he cupped the back of her neck. He leaned down to kiss her again.

She whimpered softly as he swept his tongue inside her mouth then groaned louder, her hands clinging to his arms as he deepened the kiss. He couldn't seem to get enough of her. She tasted sweet like warm vanilla and he craved for more. When she pressed her hardened nipples against his bare chest, he broke the kiss, raising his head to just look at her a moment. Her eyes were now a deep amber and, like his, her breathing was raspy and all he could do was look at her.

"Jacob?" Her voice was uncertain as she frowned.

Jacob gave her a smile and shook his head then leaned in to kiss her neck. With a soft sigh, she let her head fall back, giving him more access to her neck and bare shoulder. His mouth found that sweet, soft spot again, nipping at the skin, wishing he was sinking his teeth into the supple flesh, claiming her all over again. He felt his wolf stirring, surging forward to do just that, but he pushed him back and trailed kisses down her chest. Cupping her breasts, his mouth found one of her pebbled peaks and he sucked it deep into his mouth. Tessa arched her back as his tongue swirled around the hard nipple, her hands moving to his head to hold him there.

He let go of her nipple with a soft pop and moved to the other, chuckling at how she squirmed. Her moans urged him on as he sucked and teased one breast then the other before he started kissing down her stomach. He stopped and swirled his tongue around her belly button then lifted his head. Her elbows were holding her up so she could watch him. Damn, that was sexy. He gave her a wicked grin as he dropped to his knees again then reached out to undo the tight jeans she was wearing.

Slowly, he peeled them off, tugging them over her knees and pulled them off. Tossing them aside, he moved his hands up the inside of her legs, letting his fingers lightly brush over the white cotton panties she wore. Jacob remembered how the thongs she wore always matched her bra, but these panties were the sexiest things he'd ever seen. Brushing his fingers lightly across her panties, he watched her gasped softly then close her eyes and let her head fall back.

"Jacob quit teasing me." When she spoke, her voice was deeper, full of need.

"Oh, Little Wolf. I haven't even begun to tease you." Jacob leaned down and placed a kiss on her panties, inhaling the musky, sweet scent of her arousal. Raising his head, he hooked his fingers into her panties, tugging them down then just stared at her again. His Little Wolf was beautiful lying there, her red curls tumbling over her shoulders, her toned, tanned body stretched out before him.

"Before the night is over, I plan to feast upon every inch of you."

He kissed the damp curls between her legs, licking along the moist, warm folds of her sex and was rewarded with a deep moan of pleasure. It might have been three years since they'd been together, but her taste was still the same. "I've craved your taste every day we've been apart, Tessa, and now that I have you right where I want you, I'm going to dine like a starved man being given a five-course meal."

Jacob swirled the finger he'd slid into her as she'd started talking. Curving it up as he slid it in and out of her. With a wicked chuckle, he dipped his head, his tongue and teeth suckling and nibbling her clit.

Tessa's amber eyes glowed with need. She thrust her hips toward him, a low growl rumbling in her chest. "You're still teasing Jac... Oh gods, yes!"

"Mmm, so damn good."

Tessa panted raggedly, her moans filled the bedroom, encouraging Jacob to slide another finger into her, his rhythm became even faster. "Jacob... yes, harder. Oh, yes. More. I want more. I want your cock in me now!"

Ignoring her pleas, he continued to pleasure her clit, using his sense of smell while focusing all his attention on the feel of her muscles as they flexed and clamped down around his fingers. When he felt her hands threading into his hair, pulling him closer still, he knew she was ready. Sucking hard on her hard, little nub, he thrust hard into her, fingers curved to hit that sensitive bundle of nerves.

Tessa scream from the intensity of her climax. Wave after wave of it rippling through her core. Jacob had to fight to keep his fingers moving in and out of her, so lost to the pleasure as she was. The walls of her pussy convulsed, her juices coating his fingers while wave after wave of ecstasy wracked her body.

Tessa went limp beneath him, whimpering when he pulled his fingers from her. "Shh Little Wolf, I'm not even close to being done with you yet. Open your eyes and watch me lick your sweetness from my fingers."

When her eyes fluttered open, they were glazed from her climax, but she watched as he licked his fingers clean.

Chapter 7

Tessa

Oh.My.God. Tessa lay back against the mattress, her heart pounding out an erratic rhythm in her chest. Soft waves of aftershocks from her release made her body tremble. Taking several deep, shuddering breaths, she brushed the hair off her damp forehead. That had been her first orgasm in over three years. The last had been, well, with Jacob the night before he was banished. Now, her body ached, wanting more...needing more from him. How had she gone three years without this?

"My god, Jacob." Her voice low and wispy.

Jacob chuckled. "Oh, I'm not done with you yet, Little Wolf."

Lifting her head, Tessa rose up on her elbows to watch Jacob stand up and practically rip his jeans off his hips. He let the tattered denim fall to the floor a moment before he climbed up her body to stretch out on top of her. He nipped her bottom lip when she protested that she hadn't gotten a good look at him. "I haven't seen your naked body in over three years. How do I really know I want to do this? You could have gotten flabby with a beer gut and..."

He captured her lips in a hot, wet kiss, his tongue swept into her mouth, brushing against hers in a dance that their bodies seemed to remember. The sweet, tangy taste of herself on his lips felt erotic and forbidden. She moaned into the kiss, demanding more from him, selfishly taking everything he was giving her.

She whimpered when he broke the kiss and started nibbling his way across her cheek to her neck and to that spot he knew would drive her crazy. Her hands moved over his body, tracing the muscles in his arms and across his back with her fingers then brushed her hands over his ass. Closing her eyes, she tilted her neck slightly and remembered just how much she loved his ass. She had told him all the time. He was sexy in a tight pair of jeans, but he was heart-stopping when he was naked.

"I'm going to fuck you, Little Wolf," he whispered, his warm breath caressing her ears causing goosebumps to break out all over her skin. Lifting his head, he stared down at her a moment, his look unfathomable. She reached up to brush her fingers across his cheek then through his hair. Tessa knew right then that she shouldn't be doing this. She shouldn't be lying here with him, in his bed. Hell, she shouldn't even be in his house or this town. How would she survive if it all ended...again?

"Get out of your head, Tessa." Jacob's deep voice silenced hers.

Tessa blinked and focused on Jacob as he brushed his lips over hers again. She wrapped her arms around his neck and brought his lips back to hers.

The kiss started out in a desperate attempt to block out the last three years of pain and heartache, but Jacob took over and the kiss turned possessive, as if he was putting his claim on her as he'd done before. She closed her eyes, clinging to him, returning his kiss, arching her back to press her body as close to his as she could. Jacob moved his hips and she felt his hard cock pressing against her entrance.

Jacob lifted his head and Tessa opened her eyes to look up at him. "This is your last chance, Little Wolf."

"Please, Jacob. Don't stop."

He slid his cock inside her with one hard thrust, both of them groaning as he slid deep inside her. Pulling back, he thrust back inside her, growling into her ear sending a tingling sensation through her whole body. She moved with him, rocking her hips as he pulled out then slammed back into her. Each thrust was harder and went deeper inside her, her body tightening around him.

Twisting his hips as he moved, he brushed against the tiny bud of nerves deep inside her. She could feel her release spiraling up and around her. Her fingers dug deep into the muscles of his body. Arching her back, she cried out as her orgasm shattered around her, sending wave after wave of sensations coursing through her body. A moment later, Jacob growled as he slammed into her one more time before she felt his own release.

Tessa held Jacob when he slumped on top of her, both of them panting, trying to catch their breaths. Her heartbeat so hard in her chest she felt lightheaded and disoriented. Jacob finally lifted his head and she opened her eyes looking up at him. Neither spoke. They just looked at each other, listening to the racing of their hearts. Tessa felt as if she was drowning in the depths of his eyes.

She felt a sudden shift in the air and her heart tumbled over and tears sprang to her eyes. There it was. All the broken places she thought she had mended seemed to split open, needing him to fill them in again.

A single tear slid out of the corner of her eye and she closed them, unwilling to let Jacob see her tears. When she felt his lips softly kissing her closed eyelids, she knew it was too late. He had seen them.

"Look at me, Tessa."

She opened her eyes and looked up at him.

"Don't cry, baby. I didn't mean to make you cry."

Tessa took a deep breath and shook her head, caressing his cheek. "You didn't, Jacob. I just need…"

He kissed her, silencing her a moment then lifted his head. "I don't know what turn of fate brought you here, but I'm glad. I've missed you. Let me make love to you, Little Wolf. Let me love you all night until neither of us can think of anything other than each other."

She looked at him, not saying anything for a moment. Reaching up, she caressed his cheek. "I lied to you because I was afraid of losing Hannah." Jacob started to speak but she covered his lips with her fingers.

"Please, I need to say this. I know you wouldn't have taken her away from me. Logically I know that. But I couldn't lose anyone else in my life. I lost you, I lost my parents. I would die if something happened to Hannah. She was all I had left of you." Her voice broke and her throat tightened.

Jacob leaned down and kissed her softly then rolled onto the bed and pulled her close. She curled into him felt and realized that this was truly what being home felt like. She leaned up and kissed him, pouring all her needs and fears that had built up in the three years they were apart. He pulled her flush against him, returning her kiss and rolling her on her back. Wrapping her arms around his neck than ran her hands down his back. Tonight, she would let him love her until they both were satiated. Tomorrow she would over analyze all this and what the future held for them all.

Voices brought Tessa out of a deep sleep. Jacob had made good on his promise and by the time they were too exhausted to move, they had fallen asleep wrapped around each other. She opened her eyes, blinking several times to adjust to the sunlight coming in through the window across from the bed. Pulling the blankets over her head she mumbled about the man having no sense. Who put a bed so the sun shined directly on it in the morning? Jacob did apparently.

She lay there for a few more minutes listening to Hannah's small voice tell Jacob exactly how she liked her eggs scrambled with blueberries and her toast with a smile. Tessa couldn't help but grin at that. Hannah was very particular about her eggs only because her Uncle Sean made her that way. He would come over on Sunday mornings to fix them all breakfast and play with his goddaughter. Her chest tightened. She missed Sean and knew she needed to call him.

Throwing her legs over the side of the bed she searched the floor for her clothes then saw them folded on the dresser.

Frowning, she went over to them and slowly dressed. When had Jacob started folding clothes? Come to think of it, his house was pretty clean too. When did he start cleaning? Three years certainly did change people.

Tessa dressed then walked to the kitchen, stopping at the door and leaning against it to watch Jacob and Hannah. He had a dish towel wrapped around little Hannah's waist and she stood a chair next to him by the sink helping him do dishes. She was talking as only a three-year-old could when someone she liked stood still long enough to listen, and he was nodding and washing dishes. Once he'd washed a dish, he would hand it to Hannah and help her rinse it off then put it in the dish drainer.

"I never thought I'd live to see the day that you'd be doing dishes, Jacob." Both Jacob and Hannah turned around to smile at her and her heart felt like it had literally flipped over. It used to do that when Jacob would turn and smile at her unexpectedly. But now? Now it had her chest tightening almost, unexpectedly, painful. There was more than one heart at stake now. More than one life to ruin if the same reckless decisions were made as had been made before.

"Mommy?"

Tessa blinked, focusing on her daughter who stood with her soapy hands at her side watching her. Hannah always had a way of knowing when Tessa was upset or distracted or even angry. One day she'd have to explore that but for now, she plastered on a smile and walked to them. She untied the dishtowel from around her daughter's waist and dried her soapy hands as she leaned over to kiss her. Lifting her head, she turned it and smiled at Jacob, then helped Hannah down.

"You, little one, need to go up and change from your pajamas so head on up and I'll be right there." Hannah ran out of the kitchen as Tessa straightened.

"She's adorable." Tessa turned to look at Jacob.

"Thank you. I didn't do it alone, not really. We lived with my folks and, well, Sean is her Godfather." Jacob nodded as he dried his hands then turned to wrap his arms around her waist, pulling her to him. "I'll have to call Sean and ask him why he kept such important news away from me." He dipped his head and brushed his lips over hers.

She shook her head when he lifted his. "He did it for both of us. He knew there was no way you could come back to be with us. Do you guys talk all the time?"

Jacob shook his head, lifting her to sit on the counter then stepped between her legs, pinning her in with his arms. "I haven't talked to Sean for three years. He contacted me a month or so after everything but that's it." He brushed his lips over hers. "So, I was thinking while I watched you sleep last night…"

Heat creeped into Tessa's cheeks as she raised an eyebrow. "You watched me sleep? Did I snore?"

"You have the cutest little pig snort that I'd hoped you still made when you were in a deep sleep."

"I do not!"

"Oh, Little Wolf, you do too. But as I was saying, I was thinking last night. It's Sunday and the shop is closed. Why don't the three of us spend the day together. Let us get to know each other. Let me get to know my daughter."

Tessa nodded. "I think that would be fun. Is there someplace we can go and shift? Hannah has the most beautiful golden fur."

"Daughter? Since when are you a father, Jacob?"

The female voice had both of them turning their heads toward the backdoor. Tessa didn't know how long they all stood there staring at each other, but Jacob finally straightened. She turned to him and heard her words echoed back to her.

"Who is this woman, Jacob?"

The two women looked at each other as Tessa jumped off the counter. She regretted her decision the minute her feet hit the floor. She might be 5'6" but the woman standing at the back door was a good 3 or 4 inches taller than she was, and thin compared to Tessa's own stockier, athletic body. She wore a pair of shorts and a tank top with perfectly painted toes that probably matched her nails. Tessa still wore the outfit that she'd worn yesterday, her hair was a tangle of out-of-control curls that she'd yet to tame this morning, and she'd never been the type to get mani-pedi's. She'd been too busy running the fields around the pack land.

Jacob reached out to touch Tessa's arm, but she jerked it away, stepping out of reach. "Jacob. Who is this woman? I know she's not a member of your family because I know everyone in your family."

Jacob glanced at her then at the other woman then back to Tessa. "Tessa, this is Lorna. Lorna, what are you are you doing here?"

Lorna crossed her arms, attitude apparent the way she stood there, boring holes into Jacob's head. "I thought I'd give you a few days to cool off so we could talk. Now I see how you let off some of your temper."

Tessa knew that last comment was directed at her, which had her wolf raising its head and growling low in her chest. Tessa may feel like the woman might possibly have a point, but not her wolf. To her wolf, she had every right to be by Jacob's side, he was her mate. Jacob did grab her arm then, pulling her back against him. Tessa struggled but he only tightened his grip on her.

"Lorna, we said all we needed to say."

"I think that after two years, there were would be more to say."

Tessa lifted her chin and jerked out of Jacob's hold, her eyes burning from unshed, angry tears and backed away. "I think the two of you need to talk. I'll be with my daughter."

Chapter 8

Jacob

Jacob heard Tessa running up the stairs the minute she had left the kitchen. It may have been three years since they'd seen each other, but he still knew her. If he didn't get Lorna out of the house sooner rather than later, she'd find a way for her and Hannah to leave. If she left, then all the plans he'd made while he watched her sleep would have been for nothing.

"So that's Tessa? You didn't mention a daughter." Lorna walked past Jacob, ignoring the dark look in his eyes, not seeing their color change back and forth between man and wolf. This woman stood between his wolf and its mate and their pup. That was a very dangerous place to be. But Jacob had to remember, though, that Lorna was human, not a wolf or subject to pack laws. She really had no clue how much danger she could be in.

Lorna poured herself a cup of coffee then turned to look at him while she took a sip. "Listen, Lorna. We said all we needed to say three days ago. You wanted more, and I told you I couldn't give you more. You didn't like that and made an ultimatum. I told you we were through."

She closed her eyes a moment, setting the cup on the counter, and took a deep, shuddering breath. Opening her eyes, she looked at Jacob, tears swimming in her eyes. "All I wanted was for you to tell me you loved me. I wanted to move in, not get married. Do you recognize the difference?"

Jacob scrubbed a hand down his face then dropped into a chair at the small kitchen table where, not an hour before, he had fed and talked to his daughter. She had told him about running through the same field that he had run at her age. She couldn't stop talking about her Uncle Sean. He would give his old friend a piece of mind once he convinced Lorna to leave and explain things to Tessa. He hoped Tessa listened better than Lorna.

Lorna sat down at the table across from him, a single tear falling down her cheek. He let out a long sigh and reached over to squeeze her hand. "Lorna, I understand that you weren't asking for marriage but to me, to my family, it would be the same thing. Plus, I told you. There was only one woman that I would ever love the way you want me to love you."

Lorna jerked her hand away and looked past him toward the door. "Tessa. You will never love me the way you love Tessa."

His wolf growled low, but he pushed him down. Lorna couldn't understand why he would never love her. She wasn't his true mate. She didn't have his heart. His wolf would have no other mate once he'd found his true fated mate. He had found Tessa when she was a young, gangly sixteen-year-old. From their first kiss, they'd both known, just as their wolves had known instinctively, they belonged together.

They would have gone through the full mating ceremony, but Tessa's parents had said that, even at eighteen, she was too young. He had planned for them to do the ceremony after he had challenged Sean for Alpha. Once fully mated, there was nothing Tessa's parents could say. But that didn't happen. He lost, and they banished him. He had only said goodbye to his parents, but Tessa's screams, calling his name, echoed in his ears and his mind for three years. Last night, those screams had been replaced with her screaming his name as she found her release.

"Are you even listening to me, Jacob?"

Jacob shook his head. "Lorna, I care about you. I really do. You are important to me."

Lorna stood and wrapped her arms around herself and paced, the tears flowing freely. "I love you, Jacob. I know you care for me. Had she not shown up, I truly believe that we would have a different conversation."

He had to admit that she had him on that. Before he had gotten the call about a stranded vehicle, he'd been thinking about how he might work things out with Lorna. He kept asking himself if he was willing to throw away almost two years of what had been, until the past week, a good relationship. Lorna was sexy and sweet and a lot of fun. She made Jacob laugh and that had been huge for him. But he had gotten that call, and it had been Tessa and his daughter. He didn't mess with fate.

"Can you deny that, Jacob?"

Jacob looked at her, his heart twisting as he watched her tears, and shook his head. "No, I can't deny that. But Lorna..."

He didn't finish his sentence before she rushed to him and wrapped her arms around him laying her head on his chest. Habit had him wrapping his arms around her, holding her. She lifted her head and the next thing he knew she was kissing him, her arms tightening around his neck when he tried to pull back. He didn't want to hurt her, but the more he tried to push her away, the tighter she hung on.

The growl coming from behind them had Lorna finally unwrapping herself from him. He turned to see Tessa standing at the door with her phone in her hand; the color drained from her face. She looked between him and Lorna, her eyes widening, brows furrowed for a moment. Shaking her head in disbelief, Tessa brought the phone she held to her ear.

"Thank you, Mr. Charles, for getting back to me. I'm glad the card works now. I'll be using it today to get back to my trip."

No one said a word for a moment, but Lorna wrapped herself around him as if staking her claim. They all stood there watching each other before Tessa turned and ran up the stairs, taking two at a time. Jacob struggled to untangle himself from Lorna's arms. He didn't want to hurt her, but she wasn't cooperating. He finally wrapped his hands around her wrists, squeezing harder than he'd like, and pulled her arms from him and set her away from him.

"Lorna." Her name came out as a deep growl, his wolf very close to the surface. "We will not get back together. I need you to understand that and respect it."

Jacob stepped back, his jaw tight and his expression hard and cold. Lorna was precariously close to meeting his wolf. The two were juggling for position and Jacob felt he might lose the struggle at any moment.

"Fine." This time Lorna's tears had no effect on him. She took a deep shuddering breath. "I'm leaving. Let me know when I can get my things." Turning on her heels, she held her head high and walked out the back door.

Jacob didn't wait a second. He was already bounding up the stairs before the back-screen door banged shut. He'd been right. When he walked into the room Tessa had used to put her things, she was shoving Hannah's toys into their bags. He said nothing at first but just watched her. With his wolf's hearing he could hear her mumbling to herself and it was all he could do not to smile. This was a serious moment, and he hoped she'd listen to him.

"Tessa?"

Tessa stopped and whirled around with her wolf's growl, fire in her eyes. Man, she was sexy when she was angry. Jacob shook that off and stepped further in the room. He could hear Hannah in her room playing, talking to one of her dolls, so the two of them would have a few minutes alone.

"Where's your girlfriend? Waiting patiently for you downstairs while you take care of your past? Well, no worries, I'm almost packed. The card is working so we can go back to the hotel, and I can pay for the part so we can get out of here. You won't have to worry. I'm almost packed."

She turned back to the closet to get the rest of Hannah's things, then carried them to the bed, putting them in a bag. Turning around back to Jacob, she took a step back when she saw him even closer to her.

"Lorna left, and she's not coming back. I broke it off with her the night I got to the call that you were stranded."

"Why would you do that? I saw the look on your face when she walked in. You still care about her. So why break it off if you feel that way?"

Jacob reached out to tuck a strand of her hair behind her ear, letting his fingers softly dance across her cheek. Tessa didn't stop him, but he dropped his hand, not taking any chances she'd move away from him.

"You're right. I care for her, but she wanted something from me I couldn't give her."

"What?" Her anger seemed to ebb, but she was still defensive. Stepping closer to her, he reached out again to caress her cheek, letting his hand linger.

"She wanted my heart. She wanted me to love her, and I told her I couldn't."

"Why?" This time she whispered the question.

"I told her that there was only one woman I would ever love. It didn't matter that I would never see her again. You would always have my heart and..." He swept her hair then tugged the collar of her t-shirt and looked at the mark on her shoulder, rubbing his thumb over it. "You wear my mark. All we have to do is say the words and we will be fully mated."

He felt Tessa shiver when his thumb moved over the mark, her eyes fluttering closed. Cupping the back of her neck, he pulled her closer than brushed his lips over hers. Lifting his head, he looked down at her as she opened her eyes.

"I love you, Tessa. It almost killed me when we were torn apart like we were."

"Jacob, I mourned us too, but I had to pull myself out of it because of Hannah. Then I lost my parents, and I felt so unsettled, so alone. I left the pack telling Sean that I needed something new. I never dreamed that I would find you again."

He started to speak, but she put her fingers over his lips. "Yes, I wear your mark, which is how and when I got pregnant. Yes, all we have to do is say the words to be fully mated. But we first have to think of Hannah. I don't know how she will react to suddenly having a dad. Then there is the ceremony. First, I would want Sean there and second, don't we need a sacred circle and other wolves there to witness it? Isn't it the magic of the pack that seals it?"

Jacob let out a breath and lay his forehead against hers. She was right, as far as Hannah was concerned. They didn't know how she would react or act out being told that she suddenly had a dad. Yes, they had a lot of fun at breakfast but that had been their first real interaction. It didn't mean she wanted him to be her daddy. But he had an answer for her second concern. One he knew would surprise her.

"I agree on Hannah. You two can live here and let her get used to me being around, helping to take care of her. You fell for my charms. I'm pretty sure Hannah will too." Tessa laughed, hitting him in the stomach. He couldn't resist kissing her.

"As for your other concern? The Sheriff in town is a wolf shifter. This town is full of them. His Pack owns and runs most of the businesses in town. We met when I was on the road and was passing through Grady. Everyone in town knows about them and his pack land surrounds the town. The pack has taken me in. We could do this in their circle in front of them. They would love to witness this. As far as Sean? Would he come? Especially since he's Alpha, and it's, well, me?"

Tessa smiled and nodded. "He doesn't hate you, Jacob. You guys were best friends. He understood why you challenged him and believe it or not, he's been trying for the last three years to try to circumvent the ancient laws. Yes, he did it for me and Hannah so you could come back, but he missed his friend."

Jacob wasn't so sure, but if Tessa believed then he would too. Stepping back, he took her hand then glanced into Hannah's room as she played. "I tell you what. Why don't we spend the day together as a family? Just the three of us. Maybe go visit the pack and shift, have a picnic, or whatever you two want to do."

Tessa nodded. "I think that's a good idea and sounds fun. Why don't you head down and get ready and we'll do the same here and we can all be together?"

Jacob kissed her again before he left the room, a big smile on his lips, and headed to take a shower. He had a date with his two ladies. A date that he didn't know he had been looking forward to for the last three years.

Chapter 9

Tessa

Tessa sat with her back to the passenger door and listened to father and daughter talk to each other as they headed toward the pack lodge. Jacob had been right. She had fallen for his charms, and it looked like he was winning over their daughter too. Nothing could have made her heart so full than seeing the two of them like this. Jacob glanced over at her, grinning like a kid with his first bike.

Jacob looked back to the road and Tessa straightened in her seat. They turned onto a dirt road, surrounded by cornfields, much like the main road. She watched out the window as corn stalks zipped past them.

"There certainly is a lot of corn."

Jacob chuckled beside her. "You're in the middle of Illinois, Little Wolf. What did you expect?"

She turned her head to grinned. "Do you miss the mountains?"

Jacob reached out and lifted her hand to his lips as he nodded. "I do but Max and his pack have taken good care of me and made me feel like one of them. They will love you and Hannah."

Her stomach fluttered. She hoped they would welcome them as much as Jacob thought they would. But they could do or say whatever they wanted to her. If even one of them were ugly to Hannah, then nothing would keep them safe from her. She felt Jacob's lips on her knuckles again and she turned to smile at him.

"What's on your mind, Little Wolf?"

"Honestly I'm just nervous. I don't care about me but..."

She stopped when she heard the low growl. Laughing softly, she shook her head. "I'm glad I'm not the only one to feel that way. But my wolf is nervous too. You know that I've never been this far away from the pack. I've only met a few wolves that weren't part of the pack. I don't know if I will play well with others."

Jacob laughed as he pulled to a stop next to a large farmhouse. Turning off the truck, he turned to Hannah in the backseat. "We're here!"

Hannah let out an exaggerated sigh, rolling her eyes. "Finally."

Tessa laughed as she got out of the truck and helped Hannah out, carrying her around the vehicle to stand by Jacob. "Welcome to the sassy world of Hannah."

Jacob laughed and took Hannah from her arms then lifted his daughter to sit on his shoulders.

"Hannah, do you like wolves?" He started walking toward the back of the house, Tessa following them.

"I'm a wolf, silly."

When they reached the backyard, Jacob swept her off his shoulders and set her on the group, going down on one knee in front of her. "You are?"

"Yes. So is mommy! Aren't you, mommy?"

Tessa dropped down to her knees beside Jacob and nodded. "I am and you know what?"

"What?" Tessa pulled Hannah close, so they both looked at Jacob. "Jacob is a wolf, too."

Hannah's eyes widened and looked over at Tessa. "He is?"

Tessa nodded. "Why don't we all shift and run? I'm sure your pup would love to run in those cornfields and play hide and seek with Jacob and I. Don't you think so?" Her daughter grinned and nodded. "I think so too. Why don't you show Jacob how beautiful your wolf is?"

Hannah nodded again and stepped away from Tessa. The little girl turned and smiled at Jacob before she spoke. "Abracadabra." The minute she said the word the little girl shifted into a small ball of golden fur. The pup yelped and ran around them and Jacob laughed, turning to Tessa.

"Abracadabra?"

Tessa's cheeks reddened and nodded. "That's how my father got me to shift. My mother used to laugh and tell me the story of walking into the nursery and instead of her baby girl, there was a wolf pup in the bed tearing up a stuffed toy."

The wolf pup let out a high-pitched howl then turned and started running toward the cornfields. They both laughed when she disappeared among the stalks. "I guess the game is on." Jacob winked at Tess and shifted, shaking out his dark brown fur. He turned and looked at Tessa a long moment, then ran off toward his pup.

When Tessa saw Jacob's wolf for the first in three years, it took her breath away. She knew she had fallen in love with the wolf before she'd fallen in love with the man. The two together had been a heady mixture, almost addictive. But she had never stopped loving him in the three years they had been apart. She loved him even more now that they were together again.

Tessa grinned when she heard the two people she loved most in the world running through the cornfield and her wolf was excited to join them. Who was she to deny the animal? She shifted, shaking out the snow-white fur, then lifted her head and howled. As her howl died away, she ran into the fields after her family.

Tessa opened her eyes when the truck drove over a pothole. Yawning, she looked around seeing nothing but darkness. Not unlike the night her Durango broke down and Jacob had come to rescue them. She looked over at Jacob driving, one hand on the wheel, the other covered her hand on the console between them. His touch was warm and gentle but possessive, as if he dared anyone to touch her. She could hear Hannah's soft breathing in the seat behind her. This was her family, all nestled in the cab of the truck.

"Did you have a nice little nap?"

She looked up at him, smiling and nodding.

"You snored that cute little snore you have."

Tessa shook her head as she straightened in her seat. "I do not snore."

Jacob laughed and squeezed her hand. "Oh darlin, you snore but don't worry. You're still sexy."

Tessa pulled her hand out from under his and punched him in the arm. "You should hear you snoring in the middle of the night. Trust me, that is not sexy."

He laughed harder and put two hands on the wheel. "Darlin, I'm always sexy. That's why you can't keep your hands off me."

They both laughed, and Tessa knew it was true. He was always so damn sexy that she couldn't keep her hands off him. She turned slightly, her back against her door and looked at Hannah, her head leaning back against her car seat, holding her stuffed wolf to her chest.

"So, Tessa." She looked over to Jacob. "We've not talked about it, and it's only been a few days, but will you stay? Here with me?"

Her heart sped up, beating hard in her chest at the question. She knew one of them would ask this question but, like he'd said, it had only been a few days, not even a week since she and Hannah had even come to town. So much had happened in those few days that her head was almost spinning. Then today, with them shifting as a family, had been the best time she'd had in three years save Hannah's birth.

"Jacob, I..."

"You don't have to answer that, Tessa."

She sighed and shook her head. "Jacob, look at me."

He glanced over.

"I'm not saying yes, but I'm not saying no. I want to say yes, but we both have to think about Hannah. I really think she needs a little more time to get used to the three of us together. Then we tell her you're her father and see how that goes. After that, I… we will know if it's the right thing to do." Reaching out, she touched his arm. "Being a parent sucks sometimes."

Jacob chuckled and caught her hand and squeezed. "I'm learning that, but you've done a great job. Now there's two of us. We'll figure it all out together."

Chapter 10

Jacob

Jacob stood at the bedroom door watching as Tessa read to a sleepy Hannah. They'd had a long day of fun and family time and now, his daughter could barely keep her eyes open. But he couldn't blame her. He was tired too. All he wanted was to tuck his daughter in then take her mother downstairs, strip her of the tank top and shorts she was wearing, and both of them take a shower. Once they'd let all the hot water go cold, he wanted to take her to his bed and make love to her.

He shook his head. Maybe he shouldn't think about his daughter at the same time he was thinking about what he wanted to do to her mother. Tessa closed the book she'd been reading from then tucked the blanks up to Hannah's chin before leaning down and kissing the little girl on the forehead. Hannah peaked at him over the blanks and wiggled her fingers in a little wave before closing her eyes.

Tessa set the book on the dresser and walked up to Jacob, putting her hands on his chest and leaned up to kiss him. "She'll be asleep before we even get downstairs if we're quiet."

Jacob nodded and took her hand, leading her out of the bedroom and downstairs. Once they stepped off the last stair he turned and pulled her into his arms and kissed her. He'd wanted to do this all day, but he didn't know how Hannah would have reacted. Now that they were alone, he wasn't sure he'd be able to stop. Tessa wrapped her arms around him, whimpering softly and molding herself against him.

Lifting his head, he looked down at her, his eyes were heated gold. "I want to strip you out of your clothes, put you in the shower, and wash every inch of that luscious body of yours." He brushed his lips across hers then lifted his head again. "Afterward, I'm going to take you back to bed and keep you there until at least tomorrow afternoon if not forever."

Tessa laughed. "Is that so?"

Jacob grabbed her around the waist and picked her up as she squealed then wiggled in his arms trying to get down. He buried his head in her hair, kissing and nipping at her neck causing her to laugh and wiggle more.

"Jacob! Stop!"

He laughed at her protests and carried her into his bedroom.

"Really, Jacob. I want to talk to you then, I promise, I'll let you do all kinds of nasty things to me."

He narrowed his eyes at her, giving her a playful growl, then laid her on the bed. His eyes were drawn to her breasts as she moved to sit up.

"Jacob my eyes are up here."

Jacob looked up and gave her a wolfish grin wiggled his eyebrows. "I know but it wasn't your eyes that I wanted to see."

Tessa laughed again and shook her head. "Focus, wolf. I have something important to tell you."

"Trust me, Little Wolf, you have my undivided attention."

"I decided on the way home that I think we should ask your friend if we could perform our mating ceremony with his pack." She stood from the bed. "Ok. I'm going to take a shower then head to bed…" She walked past him then looked over her shoulder. "…upstairs."

Jacob growled again. Standing he caught her in two steps picking her up again and tossing her on the bed. She laughed as she bounced until his body covered hers, keeping her in place.

"Now what were you saying?"

She laughed again and lifted her head to kiss him. "I'm saying yes. Yes, to finishing the ritual, yes to being with you always, yes to everything."

Jacob's expression softened as a weight lifted from his shoulders. He hadn't taken for granted that she would automatically say yes when he'd asked her to go through the ceremony. He'd hoped she would, of course, but he knew she had been thinking of her daughter when she'd hesitated to give him an answer before.

"What about telling Hannah?"

"I still want to wait. I can't imagine that we'll have the ceremony the minute you talk to your friend. We'll all spend time together as a family like we talked about, and you can still win her over with her charms."

Jacob grinned then kissed her. She parted her lips for him, and he deepened the kiss, taking everything she offered to him. His chest tightened at the emotions he felt from her. This was his woman, his mate, his love. He would never let her go again.

He lifted his head, and she slowly opened her eyes, reaching up to caress his cheek. He leaned into her touch then turned his head to kiss her palm. "I love you, Tessa. I never stopped."

Tessa nodded and brushed her fingers through his hair. "I love you, too, Jacob and I never stopped. It nearly killed me to lose you, but I never stopped loving you. We will have what we should have had. We will have a life together and a family together."

"Will you be ok with not returning to Colorado? I don't think marrying me will endear you to the Elders, nor do I think they will welcome me back with open arms."

She grinned. "I've become quite fond of cornfields. I think we will live a long life here."

Jacob matched her smile and nodded. I agree. Hannah will love it here too, and there are lots of pups she'll be able to play with. She won't be bored. I promise."

Chapter 11

Tessa

Tessa put the last three pancakes on a platter then set it on the table as she sat down. Jacob stabbed one with his fork and put it on Hannah's plate then took the other two for himself. She sat watched them both, a smile tugging at her lips. Hannah was rambling as only a three-year-old could, and Jacob was listening attentively while he put a little butter and syrup on her pancake.

They had been doing the same thing for over a week. She didn't know exactly when it happened. When had they fallen into such a comfortable routine? When had they fallen into a routine of, well, a family? They were acting like a family even though the mating ceremony wasn't for another couple of weeks, and they had yet to tell Hannah that Jacob was her father.

"Well, ladies, I have to get to work." Jacob stood, leaned down and kissed the top of Hannah's head then looked at Tessa. She followed him to the back door to kiss him goodbye when he wrapped his arms around her, pulling her so close that her body molded into his. "I love you, Little Wolf. You know that right?"

Tessa smiled and nodded, her hand moving up his hard chest to cup the back of his neck. He leaned down and captured her lips in a soft, wet kiss. Pulling back, she opened her eyes to see him looking down at her with determination.

"I want you to think about something today." He brushed his lips over hers again.

"What?"

"I want you to think about us telling Hannah that I'm her father."

Tessa's stomach started churning and she put a shaking hand on it. She didn't know why she was nervous about telling Hannah. She deserved to know that the man she had become so attached to was her father. Jacob deserved it. He was so loving and protective of his little girl that it sometimes brought tears to Tessa's eyes seeing them together. He was right to ask.

Taking a deep breath, she pushed down her anxiety and gave him a shaky smile. "You're right. I think it's time."

The smile he gave her was well worth ignoring her anxiety. It had her heart skipping a beat then start hammering in her chest. When he touched her arms, an electric jolt shot straight through her, straight to her core, ramping up her need for him. If she'd known she'd get that smile from him, she would have agreed to tell Hannah sooner.

"I love you, Tessa." Jacob leaned in to whisper in her ear, his warm breath sending goosebumps over her. "I want to stay home do very dirty things to my Little Wolf."

Tessa struggled to take a breath, her thighs quivering from the throbbing between her legs. "Jacob, please."

He chuckled in her ear before straightening. "Tonight. After we talk to Hannah then we put her to bed, you are mine. I plan to devour you until you are spent and shaking then do it all over again." He kissed her forehead then turned and left her standing there looking after him.

Tessa didn't know how she managed to turn from the back door and go to Hannah, but she did, acutely aware of how the shorts she wore rubbed against her with every step she took. Damn him.

She helped Hannah down from the table then took her upstairs to give her a bath. She'd managed to get syrup in her hair. How had she gotten syrup in her hair? Tessa shook her head as she rinsed Hannah's hair, got her out of the tub, dry her off then let her go play in her room.

Tessa was getting dressed when her phone rang. Picking it up, she smiled when she saw Sean's name. She had called him to tell him about the mating ceremony, and how she wanted him there but had to leave a message.

"Sean!" Tessa sat down on the bed, a big smile on her face.

"Tessa, hi." Her smile slowly faded at the tone of his voice. "I got your message. I'm happy you were able to find Jacob after all this time."

"Why don't you sound like it?" Her hold tightened on her phone waiting to hear what he was calling about, dreading what he was going to say.

There was silence on his end before he sighed. "I'm at the back door, Tessa. Can you come let me in?"

Confused, she ended the call without a word and put her t-shirt on before hurrying to the back door. She opened it and frowned, her eyes narrowing when she saw not only Sean but two of the pack enforcers standing behind him. "What's going on, Sean?"

"Can we please come in? We need to talk."

Tessa frowned and pushed the screen door open for them. Without saying a word, she turned from the door and walked to the kitchen table sitting down. Leaning back in the chair with her arms crossed, the three of them took the other chairs then they all were silent. Staring down the two enforcers until they started to shit in the seats, she finally turned her attention to Sean.

"Spit it out, Sean. Why are you here? I know it's not because you're suddenly worried about me or that you want to be part of the mating ceremony."

Adrenaline seemed to shoot through her body as her stomach started to churn and she struggled to catch a breath. She closed her eyes as the world seemed to spin around her until she clinched her fists and forced herself to take several deep breaths to calm herself. This was Sean. No matter what the reason he was here, he wouldn't hurt her or Hannah. In fact, he'd give his life protecting them. She needed to give him the benefit of the doubt and see what he wanted.

"I'm sorry, Sean. I don't mean to get so snippy with you. I just don't... "

Sean cut her off from whatever else she was going to say, dropping a bomb on her she'd never expected from him. "Tessa you need to come back and I mean right away."

"Why? What's happened? Sean, spit it out. Has someone died?"

Tessa's stomach started to hurt, churning and burning. She remembered the day she had gotten the call about her parents. For the second time in three years, her whole world had caved in on her. Now, as her heart started beating faster and she struggled to breathe, she felt helpless in stopping that happening to her again.

"The Elders are threatening to banish you if you don't come back."

She sat there, Sean's voice echoing in her ear only drowned out slightly by the loud beating of her heart. Shaking her head in confusion, she blinked several times before she spoke. "I'm sorry? Why would I be banned? I don't understand?"

"Jacob's not only banned, but everyone in the pack is forbidden to have any contact with him."

"Why didn't you tell me that? Why didn't I ever know that?"

Sean scrubbed a hand down his face and sighed. "I never in a million years thought you'd find him. Hell, I lost track of him, so how could I know you'd breakdown where you did? What were the odds that he would be the one to come to help you?"

Tears burned the back of her eyes and she blinked rapidly to keep the tears from falling. What did life have against her? Was she not allowed to be happy? Disbelief was replaced with anger as she pushed away from the table, standing and started to pace. "I don't understand, Sean? My god, my family is one of the founding members of the pack. They can't banish me."

"They can and will, Tessa. I said the same thing to them, but they promptly informed me that they will wipe your family name out of the historical records of the pack. It will be as if the family were never members, founding or not."

Tessa stopped her pacing and stared at him, words failing her. Her great grandfather, Aidan Cafferty had been Sean's great grandfather's best friend and had come over from Ireland with him. They had married sisters and made the trek out west to find a better life. Both families had flourished and opened their arms to any wolf who needed a pack. Both families were the foundation of the pack, their history.

Her father had been very proud of his family's heritage and place in the pack hierarchy. She would sit with him, enthralled by the stories he'd tell and even now, she could tell the same stories word for word to Hannah. If the Elders did what they were threatening to do, there wouldn't be any stories to tell her daughter. Tears filled her eyes as she dropped back down in the chair she'd vacated earlier.

"Sean, they can't do that." She looked at him pleading. "You're the alpha. Can't you do something? Can't you…"

Sean shook his head, reaching out to touch her hand. "I tried." Tear filled his own eyes and he squeezed her hand. "I swear I tried, Tessa. But you know that when it comes to the history of the pack and keeping the traditions and laws, they have the final say on something like this."

Tessa dropped her head into hands then scrubbed her hands down her face. When she looked back up tears streaked down her cheeks. "How did they find out, Sean? How did they know where I was?"

Sean took a deep breath, letting it out slowly. "The alpha of Jacob's new pack reached out because of the mating ceremony. It was out of common courtesy because that would make you a part of their pack too."

Her heart sank. They never thought that would happen. It felt as if the fates didn't want them to be together. It felt as if they were doomed to never be together and be happy.

"Tessa you have to come back with me now. Right now. The Elders were going to send the enforcers after you and were ordered to kidnap you and Hannah if they had to. I was able to at least stop that from happening. But I have less than forty-eight hours to get you back, which means we have to leave right now." She shook her head. There was no way she could just pick up and leave without talking to Jacob. She wouldn't do that. She…couldn't do that.

"I know what you're thinking, and I know I'm asking for the impossible. But I swear, Tessa if you come with me right now, I'll find a way for you and Jacob to be together." Tessa just stared at him, tears flowing freely now as her heart shattered into a million pieces.

Her throat hurt as she spoke, her words coming out as sobs. "I'll go pack what little I've unpacked. Hannah is asleep upstairs. Can you go get her, Sean? Your guys can get the rest of our luggage and put it all into the Durango. If I have to leave, I want to do it right now before Jacob comes home."

Tessa pushed away from the table, not looking to see if Sean or his men were getting up too. She didn't care. She walked into Jacob's room and closed the door behind her, falling face-first onto the bed and sobbing. When her tears were finally spent, she grabbed the few things that she had moved into the bedroom and packed them in her bag.

When she finished, she found the notebook and pen she'd seen sitting on the dresser earlier and sat down. She wrote Jacob a note, or letter considering the length. Pouring all her love and finally regret into the words, she told him one last time how much she loved him then folded the papers, putting them on his pillow.

Standing, she looked around the bedroom. Pushing away all the dreams she'd had of their future together, she saw the shirt he'd worn the day before sitting on top of his hamper. Going to it, she picked it up and brought it to her nose, inhaling the pure, earthy scent that was all Jacob then put it into her bag. She needed something this time. Something that would help her remember his scent as she fell asleep in it.

Opening the bedroom door, she saw Sean standing in the kitchen with Hannah still asleep in his arms. "Ready?"

Tessa rubbed her daughter's back, nodded, then turned away from him and headed outside to her Durango. One of the Enforcers who had come with Sean was shutting the back of the vehicle and looked at Sean. She opened the back door so he could put his goddaughter in her car seat, then slid into the passenger side of the vehicle. Sean got in behind the wheel and started the Durango. Out of the corner of her eyes, she saw him look at her, but she refused to look at him. Letting out a sigh, he put it into gear, pulling out of Jacob's driveway and out of town. Leaving her heart and soul behind them.

Chapter 12

Jacob

Jacob walked into his kitchen, stopping long enough to take his oil-covered boots off, then looked around. The silence in the house was almost deafening as he moved through the kitchen and to the living room. He had expected to hear Hannah's laughter from somewhere in the house or to hear Tessa singing softly to her daughter. That's what he'd been coming home to, it was the reason he had been coming home instead of going to the bar like he used to. Having Tessa and Hannah around had truly made his house a home.

Frowning, he went into his bedroom to change. Maybe they had run to the store or were at the park. He stripped out of his dirty coveralls, tossing them into the hamper then grabbed a pair of jeans and t-shirt from the dresser. He was leaving the room but saw the folded piece of paper sitting on his pillow. Reaching the bed in a single stride, he grabbed the note and opened it. After reading a few lines, he slowly sank to the bed.

Tessa talked about how much she loved him and how much she had wanted all of them to be a family. He was and always would be the love of her life, her soul, her fated mate, but sometimes duty had to come before everything else.

Jacob growled as he continued to read. The pack. The fucking pack. The same pack that had thrown him out and turned their backs on him was trying to do the same thing to her and Hannah. There was one difference, he knew. Tessa's family were one of the founding families, their history was intertwined with everything that the pack used to be and still was. She had to leave to save her family. Hannah needed that history.

Crumbling the piece of paper, Jacob let out another growl knowing his wolf was near the surface. His mate. Their mate was gone...again. The pain in his chest nearly brought him to his knees as anger and grief gripped his body. He had survived losing his mate once. He did think neither he nor his wolf was going to survive it again.

Tessa had said that Sean and a couple of his enforcers had come and taken them away. But how had Sean known? How had the elders known where she was and who she was with? Max. His best friend's name echoed in his mind. Max was the sheriff in town and Alpha of the local pack. The same pack that had taken him in and gave him a home when he'd lost everything. But why would he say anything? How would he know who to tell?

Jacob stuffed the crumpled piece of paper into his pocket and pulled out his phone. Hitting speed dial, he waited for Max to answer but it went to voicemail. "Where the fuck are you? She's gone. She's fucking gone. What did you do?"

He stabbed at the phone to disconnect it and stuffed it back into his pocket. Looking around the room, he saw a shirt on the chair across the room. Moving to it, he knew even before he grabbed it that it was one of Tessa's shirts. He could smell her. Honeysuckle and jasmine combined, filling him with her. It only took him a few moments before the decision hit him. He was going after her, and no one was going to stop him from getting his mate...no...his family back.

Grabbing a few things, he stuffed them into his pack and headed to the kitchen. He walked out the back door, pulling his leather jacket on as the door slammed shut behind him. Looking up, he saw Max walking out of the garage, his face expressionless but Jacob could tell by the set of his jaw, his friend had come to talk to him about all this.

"What the fuck have you done, Max? She's gone. They took her."

His words hit the sheriff, stopping him in his tracks. He dropped down onto one of the chairs on the patio. Scrubbing his hand down his face, Max shook his head. "I swear, Jacob, I didn't know she would be taken or leave."

Jacob looked at him before dropping his pack and sitting down across from him. He and Tessa had sat like this just last night playing with their daughter. He ignored the crushing of his heart and looked at Max. "What happened was the pack alpha, Sean O'Reilly, and a couple of his enforcers came to get Tessa and Hannah. What did you do?"

Max took his time looking at Jacob but when he did, he let out a breath before he spoke. "It's courtesy that one pack communicates with another when doing the mating ceremony if one of the wolves in the ceremony is not part of their pack. I left it up to my father to do it and, instead of calling the alpha, he must have called one of the elders. He is very old school. The elders of a pack are everything to him."

Jacob dropped his head for a moment. He couldn't be angry at Max or his father for following pack protocol. He knew all too well how the workings of a pack can control each member. Like with him. Yes, he had understood the consequences of challenging Sean for Alpha, but he hadn't truly thought he'd be completely banned. He thought he'd be forbidden from participating in certain pack ceremonies or, at the most, be banished to the outer edges of the pack land. He hadn't dreamed that they would truly make him leave without even being able to say goodbye to Tessa.

"What is going to happen to her?" Max asked penetrating Jacob's thoughts.

Jacob shook his head. "Tessa's great grandfather was one of the founding members of the pack. He had come across from Ireland with Sean O'Riley's great grandfather looking for the proverbial better life. Several families had come with them. They all made their way to Colorado and decided to stay. They formed the pack. The elders are threatening to erase all trace of Tessa's family name from the history of the pack. They are forbidding her to have anything to do with me because I was banished."

His friend cursed and shook his head. "I swear Jacob…"

Jacob held up his hand. "You didn't know. Hell, neither of us knew something like this would happen. Tessa and I spoke about it, and we knew the pack wouldn't be happy, but we never thought they'd go this far to prevent our mating."

"What are you going to do?"

He looked down at his pack and back to his friend. "I'm going to get my fucking family back." He stood and grabbed his pack. "I refuse to let those bastards pull us apart again."

Max stood and nodded reaching out to squeeze Jacob's shoulder. "If you need back up, you call me. YOUR pack will come to help you."

Emotions swept over Jacob as he nodded. He had truly made a home here with a pack who cared about him and had opened their arms to him. "Thanks man. I have you on speed dial."

Max chuckled. "Then go and get your mate back. Bring your family home where they belong."

Jacob had been riding for a couple of days before he finally turned off the highway onto the Forest Access road that would take him to the pack's lodge. He was nervous and on edge. He had stopped by Tessa's place but she nor Hannah were there. The only place he could think they'd be was with Sean at the Lodge. That thought had his wolf lifting its head and growling. It had taken him a few minutes to calm his beast. There was nothing going on between Tessa and Sean. Neither had ever seen each other that way.

The sun had slipped behind the peaks and the sky was darkening the closer he got. He smelled the burning wood before he even saw the bonfire. Fear gripped him as he sped up. Memories of that fateful night flooded his mind. He didn't want Tessa to face the same fate as he had and he would be damned if anyone hurt her.

When he pulled up and stopped just inside the tree line, he could see the pack gathered, several in wolf form but no sign of Tessa or Hannah. He could feel the solemnness of the pack, even from where he stood. There was no laughter, no hum of conversations like there normally would be. That, if anything, caused him alarm.

Jacob moved around to the Lodge, trying to stay downwind as he went. He didn't want to be discovered before he found Tessa and if not her, then Sean. He managed to make it to the back of the Lodge before he scented her. Slowly, and as quietly as he could, he made his way to the back door to the Lodge then opened it, stepping inside. Tessa's scent instantly surrounded him, and her voice echoed on the air to him. She was angry and hurt. He could tell in her voice. He had to comfort his mate. He had to protect her from whatever the fools of this pack were going to throw at her.

"Sean this is bullshit. They can't throw me out. They wouldn't dare wipe my family name from everything. Half this pack is related to me. Are they just going to erase them too?"

Jacob made it to Sean's office where he could see her pacing, her hands waving in the air as she spoke. She started to speak again, but Sean held his hand up, his head lifting slightly as if he were sniffing the air. Jacob knew then that Sean had scented him, so instead of staying outside the office, he walked in as if he'd owned the place.

"Jacob." He gave Tessa a reassuring smile and looked at Sean as he moved to stand between them.

"You're really going to stand between a wolf and his mate?"

Sean stared at him, arms crossed and unmoving. "I could kill you right here and now Jacob, and I would be in my perfect right to do so."

Jacob raised an eyebrow and crossed his own arms. "And is that what you plan to do, Sean? Kill me? We were best friends once, the three of us inseparable. We were like brothers. You going to kill your brother?"

He saw the minute Sean backed down, his body slumping slightly as he shook his head, walking past Sean to close and lock the office door. Once he was no longer between them, Tessa ran to Jacob, wrapping her arms around him and burying her head in his neck when he lifted her. He had known she hadn't left willingly, but this only proved it.

"Jacob, I'm sorry I left. I had to."

"Sshh its ok, Little Wolf. I got your letter. I understand." He gave a hard look at Sean then. "What I don't understand is how you, as Alpha, would allow this bullshit to happen."

Sean sat behind his desk and leaned back to watch them. Jacob lowered Tessa to the floor, and she turned to look at Sean, but he wasn't willing to let her away from him. "We've been looking through everything to find a way around all this. But we've come up with nothing."

That was when Jacob saw all the books and journals laying around the room. The place was piled with them on every table space available, even on the floor. He looked at Sean. "What about the original charters?"

Sean and Tessa looked at him then at each other. "No one has thought to check the original charters. Do you even know where they're kept?"

Sean got up from behind his desk, walked to the far end of his office, and pushed on one side of the bookcase. It slowly swung open to reveal a large safe. Jacob and Tessa moved up behind him as he worked the combination, then opened it, the door creaking in protest. They all looked inside the safe, none saying a word at first. "What are all those journals, Sean?"

"Those are all my great grandfather's journals, the first charters and subsequent changes up until my grandfather's death. My father never updated them and let the pack just move on with what was last written."

Jacob pushed past him and grabbed a couple of journals and handed one to Tessa. "I suggest we get to reading."

Sean looked at the clock then at the two of them. "We better hurry. We have an hour before the elders gather at the bonfire. Let's hope we find something before then."

Chapter 13

Tessa

Tessa looked out at the crowd, their voices a low hum mixing with the sounds of the forest. She had always loved those sounds. She and Jacob would lay on the ground for hours listening to them, talking about their future together. But, as she looked at her pack around the fire, their future hadn't worked out quite like they'd dreamed.

"Can everyone please gather around now?" Sean's booming, alpha tone had her shaking off the memories of her and Jacob and turning her attention to the crowd gathering closer around the huge bonfire. "As many of you know, almost four years ago Jacob Murphy and I fought for alpha position. Jacob lost, barely if I had to admit. He almost had me. Since he lost, Jacob was banished from the pack."

Tessa looked over to the Lodge, and it gave her strength to see Jacob standing there watching her. He gave her one nod which she returned. She knew what he was saying with that nod and would take it to heart.

"Had Jacob remained with the pack, he and Tessa Cafferty would have been mated. As it were, Hannah, whom we all love and adore, is a result of their partial mating. After the deaths of Tessa's parents, she took Hannah away for a while to gather herself, which I supported.

Along the way, she met back up with Jacob quite by accident. But was it an accident? Or was it Fate herself putting them together, knowing they were fated mates."

The crowd started talking in hushed tones again and Tessa strained to hear them, but Sean started speaking again.

"The elders got word that Tessa and Jacob had found each other and were going to do the final mating ceremony with Jacob's new pack. They have threatened to banish Tessa and wipe her family's name from the history of the pack."

The crowd grumblings started getting louder and Sean worked to quiet them down. "Tessa is here to defend herself to the elders and the pack. I ask that she be heard." Sean stepped away from the fire, nodding to Tessa who stepped in the middle close to the fire and turned toward the group of men gathered. They all thought they had full-deciding ability of what went on in the pack. Boy was Tessa gonna prove them wrong. Her eyes moved to two of them. They were her second cousins. When they refused to meet her gaze, she sighed and shook her head.

"Many of you may think that I'm here to defend myself in this decree by our Elders. You would be wrong. I am here to remind the Elders that my great-grandfather, Aiden Cafferty was one of the founding members of this pack. I am related to half of this pack in one way or another. If they remove my name, my family's name, from its history, they remove your name as well. Everything you've done for this pack will be forgotten."

Tessa stopped a moment, watching the crowd, hearing their mumbled voices. No one, not one of them, had thought of that. She looked over her shoulder at the two elders standing behind her then turned fully around, addressing them personally. "Charles and Michael, you are my second cousins, my family. Whether or not you vote for this decree, you will no longer be able to serve as elders to the pack. Have you even thought of that?" By the looks on their faces she could tell that the thought hadn't even crossed their minds.

"I stand with Tessa." She whirled around at the sound of Jacob's voice but couldn't see him. Sean had heard him too and turned looking for him then caught Tessa's eye, nodding toward the pack.

Turning, Tessa was stunned, her mouth dropping a moment before she closed it again. The pack was dividing itself, parting slowly until her family, anyone with Cafferty blood running through their veins moved to one side. When everyone had divided, only a few families stood on her left but most of the pack stood to her right.

"Tessa is right. If you erase the Cafferty name from the pack's history, then there is no pack." Sean stepped in front of the larger crowd, crossing his arms over his large chest.

"You are the Alpha." One of the Elders stepped forward. "You sat that there and agreed with our decision"

Sean laughed shaking his head. "Your memory is slipping on you, Charles. I sat there and told you it was ridiculous, and it wouldn't stand up with the Pack. What I did agree to was that it be me who went to bring Tessa home."

Tears filled Tessa's eyes as she gave Sean a watery smile. How had she doubted him? Then she looked around the gathering but didn't see Hannah nor Jacob. He had told her that he was going to get her from one of Tessa's cousins then come back to the gathering, but she didn't see them. She prayed that he wasn't seen by anyone except her cousin. She hoped he wasn't locked up, but then where was Hannah.

Her heart started to beat frantically in her chest, her eyes darting around the crowd then skimming the tree line. Where were they? She looked to Sean and he shook his head as if he'd read her mind. Frowning, she reached in her pocket for her phone then remembered she had left it on Sean's desk. Just her luck!

A true panic attack was starting to hit her until she heard the pack starting to talk, the noise level getting higher. Turning she saw Jacob walking out of the trees carrying their daughter. Several enforcers stepped up, stopping him. She watched as Jacob looked over at Sean then the Enforcers. "Let him pass."

Without a glance to Sean again, the Enforcers stepped aside, and Jacob carried Hannah to stand next to Sean. He looked at Tessa and gave her his sexy, half smile where just the corner of his mouth lifted but his eyes twinkled. She smiled wide until one of the Elders spoke up.

"That wolf was banned from the pack three years ago. What is he doing here? Why haven't the Enforcers escorted him off pack land before now?"

Tessa turned. "The original doctrine that was signed by all the founding families state that a mate to one of the Cafferty's cannot be banned. They can be reprimanded, but they cannot be banned. Jacob and I are mated. Our daughter, Hannah, is proof of that. We still need to complete the ceremony, but we are mated."

"What original doctrine? We were under the impression that the founding contract and all the journals were gone. Moved through the years to the point that no one knows where they are."

"My father found them and kept them in his safe." Sean finally stepped up to stand by Tessa's side. "I will make sure these are available for the whole pack to read, but I looked through them before this meeting. My father put too much faith and power in the hands of the Elders. The original doctrine clearly states what the Elders can and cannot do. Up until now, I didn't realize what he did. I do now."

"As Alpha of the Wolf Creek Pack, I order each Elder to take the time to review everything that we've found and familiarize themselves with everything. As Alpha, I revoke your ruling that banishes Jacob from the pack, hence Tessa is no longer in danger of losing everything you wanted to take away from her."

Chapter 14

Jacob

Jacob woke and listened to the sounds around him. Tessa lay next to him, curled into his side, snoring softly. He could hear Hannah in her room, mumbling softly in her sleep, but outside, he didn't hear anything. His wolf instantly came to attention as Jacob slowly got out of bed, trying not to wake Tessa. She'd had a rough couple of days, they all had, and she needed to get her rest.

Grabbing his jeans and t-shirt, he walked into the living room and put them on, then went to the front door, opening it. Jacob stepped out onto the front porch, the night air chilly and the wood cold under his feet. The forest around Tessa's place was quiet. Eerily quiet. Someone or something was close by but he could scent anything.

Jacob growled when he saw the dark figure approaching the house. The figure stopped a moment and shined a flashlight to its face. Jacob relaxed when he saw Sean, shaking his head and running his hands through his hair.

"Fuck, Sean. I was about to shift and tear you apart."

Sean chuckled as he walked up the steps to the porch. "You didn't beat me the last time. What makes you think you could beat me now?

Jacob laughed then sat down in one of the chairs Tessa had on the porch, Sean dropping down in one beside him. "Too soon, man. Too soon to bring that shit up."

Sean laughed with him and nodded. "You got that right."

"What fucking time is it by the way?"

Jacob watched Sean shrug. "It's early. Maybe around 4:00."

"Jesus, Sean. What are you doing here so early? Tessa and I just got to bed maybe three hours ago."

He heard Sean chuckle then watched as he settled back into the chair as if he were staying in that spot for a while. Jacob sighed and settled back too. Might as well get comfortable and listen to whatever it was Sean had felt the need to get up so early and come talk to him about.

"I want you to know I looked for you. I even hired a private investigator."

Jacob couldn't have been more shocked by that statement. The two of them had been like brothers growing up together, running through the meadows and forest surrounding the compound. Then there was three of them. Tessa had been bored one day and was following her older cousin around, irritating him and bugging him until he agreed that she could go with him and Jacob.

Those had been the fun days, Jacob thought. The days they were free without a care in the world. Things didn't get complicated until Jacob and Tessa discovered they were fated mates. They'd spent more and more time together as a couple and the times that Sean would join them became few and far between.

"I covered my tracks pretty well. Once it actually sank in that I would never be able to get to Tessa, I started covering my tracks, zig zagging across the country, taking on different names until I rode into Grady, Illinois. I was tired of being on the road and had gotten a hotel room then went to the bar across from the hotel. That's where I met Max Tucker, Sheriff and Alpha. After a couple of beers, he convinced me to stay."

Sean nodded and they fell silent a moment. The horizon was starting to turn a bluish red and the forest was coming alive. This was one thing Jacob had missed living in Illinois. Colorado had the most beautiful sunrises and sunsets. Illinois offered him cornfields. Although beautiful in its own right, it was not Colorado.

"What are you two doing out here?" Tessa stepped out onto the porch wearing a sweatshirt and her pajama pants and crawled onto Jacob's lap, shivering as she did.

"Go back to bed, Tessa. You don't need to be up. Sean and I were just having some guy talk."

Tessa snorted then grinned as she snuggled closer to Jacob. He wrapped his arms around her to keep her warm. "So, what kind of "guy talk." She yawned in the middle of her statement, and Jacob shook his head.

"I actually came over to talk to Jacob. I have persuaded the Elders to change their decree and you are no longer banished from the pack and it's not because you're mated to a founding family member. You weren't a danger to me when you lost. We would have still been friends. Besides it's a stupid law, and as Alpha, I've decided to make a stand and abolish it"

Jacob looked at Tessa who was looking at him with wide eyes. He could feel her heart beating hard against her chest and he started to comb through her tangled hair with his fingers. He never thought he'd be allowed to be a part of the pack again, so it wasn't something he'd dwelled on. The Grady Pack had taken him in, so he hadn't missed having a pack. The only thing he'd wanted back was in his arms right now.

"So, it'll be like he never left?" Jacob heard the hopeful note in her voice.

"Yeah it would be exactly like that."

"What if I don't want to be a part of this pack anymore? It turned its back on both of us, especially when Tessa was pregnant. How do I know it won't happen again?"

Sean and Tessa both looked at him.

"What? It's a legitimate concern."

"But it's Hannah's pack. I absolutely appreciate Max's offer to be a member of the Grady Pack, but her history is here. Maybe we all can be a part of both packs?"

Tessa looked at Sean who nodded. "I have no problem with that. I can talk to Max if you want me to."

Jacob looked at both of them then sighed, pulling Tessa a little closer so he could kiss her. If that's what Tessa wanted, then that's what he would do. She was right. This is where Hannah's history was, and she could make new memories and traditions with them in the Grady Pack as well.

"Alright but I can talk to Max. I know he won't have a problem with it. Thank you, Sean, for giving us that. I know it had to be hard to go against the Elders the way you did."

Sean stood up and lay his hand on Jacob's shoulder. "It was hard. That's why you owe me."

Jacob chuckled and shook his head. "I knew there would be a catch."

"I want you to be one of my head Enforcers. There would be two of you, and it would lessen my burden of overseeing them every day."

"Who's the other one?"

"Ben Kelly."

Jacob groaned and shook his head. "He's back? I didn't see him last night."

"Yes, he's back, but he keeps to himself. He's living in the cabin at the far west border of the pack land. I'd like to have someone closer too. You living here would be perfect."

"I'll have to think about it, Sean. I have my own shop in Grady. I'd have to figure out logistics on it."

Sean nodded as he started to leave. "Do that and get back to me. It would really be helping me out."

Jacob and Tessa sat there in silence watching Sean leaving, the sun finally sending out its first rays through the forest and the area around Tessa's home. Well, it was his home now too. Would he get used to that?

"What's going on in that overactive brain of yours, Little Wolf?"

Tessa smiled turning her head to look at him. "I'm happy."

"Are you?"

She nodded.

"Then its settled. We'll split our time between Grady and here. I'll hire a couple of guys to help me out at the shop so I can be gone."

Her smile widened, and his heartbeat quickened. How had he gotten so lucky? He had the most beautiful mate and he had the cutest, smartest daughter. When he'd been banished, he'd felt his life was over. Even after moving to Grady and starting a new life there. It was never truly satisfying, and he'd been getting restless lately. Something he'd never shared with Max or Lorna. But Fate had decided he'd had enough and had brought his life back to him. He would never do anything to jeopardize that again.

"I love you, Jacob."

Jacob focused back on Tessa and smiled. "I love you too, Little Wolf. Why don't we go back in and I'll show you just how much I love you."

Tessa grinned. "We'll have to be quick. Hannah doesn't sleep very late in the mornings."

Jacob stood, tossed Tessa over his shoulder, smacking her ass.

"Jacob! Put me down. I can walk."

"Nope. I'm not taking any chances that you get away from me again." He nipped at her hip and she laughed, squirming in his arms. He just smacked her ass and carried her inside. Hopefully he'd have enough time to do what he wanted to do to her right now. If not, there was always nap time and bedtime later. One way or another, he'd have what he wanted and what he wanted was in his arms right now.

Thanks from the Author

I hope you enjoyed reading Tessa and Jacob's story. I never intended to write them but I wanted something to kick off my debut series, Wolf Creek Pack. This story started out as a short story but as the more I wrote the more they wanted their story told. So, I gave in.

If you enjoyed reading it as much as I enjoyed writing it, it would mean a lot to me if you would leave a review. Even just a quick note on Amazon to say - Good Job, or Great Read, makes a big difference to me and my career.

You know what would really make my day? If you had such a good time reading this book that you want to know when the next book I write for you comes out.

To keep up on all my writing and everything going on in my world, join my newsletter, Strange Musings. Click here ------ >https://mailchi.mp/f137ff902447/strange-musings

You can also find me on Instagram and Twitter,.

Instagram: https://www.instagram.com/tjfinnauthor/
Twitter: https://twitter.com/TJFinn5

Join my reader's group, Strange Fates Hangout, and join in all the fun and shenanigans as well contests, guess authors and so much more. Clink the link:

https://www.facebook.com/groups/476093469611028

About the Author

TJ Finn

TJ Finn loves reading, writing, stalking other authors that she can fangirl over on Facebook, dogs, and non-hoppy beer.

She's the author of super sexy paranormal romance and can't wait to get her next book out into the world for her brand spanking new raving fans.

You can find TJ on Facebook, Twitter, Instagram, Goodreads. She loves to hear from readers and really wants you to find her on the internet so she can procrastinate writing her next one-thousand words.

Other Books by TJ Finn

Dangerous Magic - Claire and Finn must work together if they are going to protect those they love from the dangers that threaten them. Can they save everyone without losing each other, or will the voices finally drive Claire to insanity?

Dangerously Scrooged - Will the ghosts of Christmas past threaten their happiness or will they finally find the love they'd been searching for?

Dangerous Love - One day Cupid shoots his arrow. Nikka's wolf is certain Ash is her mate, but both Nikka and Ash fight their feelings and growing attraction. When her past catches up with her, getting shot by Cupid's arrow may prove deadly for them both.

Writing as D.T. Strange

<u>Fated Treasures</u> - Fianna Arden is a witch that seeks ancient lore and treasures. When she learns of Gerri Wilder's Paranormal Dating Agency, she discovers Gerri's reputation as an expert matchmaker and decides she has to look into it. After all, love is the stuff legends and lore are based off of. That and Fi needs to know how she does it. But will being matched up with jaded wolf shifter, Cameron Bishop on a mock double date end up being more than she bargained for? Or could it be possible, that a fated treasure will help both Fianna and Cameron find, not only what they are looking for, but also what they never expected to find?